When in a Hole, Stop Digging

To Celia.

Colin Goodwin

Best Wishes,

2QT Limited (Publishing)

First Edition published 2016 by
2QT Limited (Publishing)
Settle, North Yorkshire BD24 9RH United Kingdom

Copyright © Colin Goodwin 2015
The right of Colin Goodwin to be identified as the author of this work has been asserted by him in accordance with the Copyright, Designs and Patents Act 1988

All rights reserved. This book is sold subject to the condition that no part of this book is to be reproduced, in any shape or form. Or by way of trade, stored in a retrieval system or transmitted in any form or by any means, electronic, mechanical, photocopying, recording, be lent, re-sold, hired out or otherwise circulated in any form of binding or cover other than that in which it is published and without a similar condition, including this condition being imposed on the subsequent purchaser, without prior permission of the copyright holder.

This is a work of fiction and any resemblance to any person living or dead is purely coincidental. The place names mentioned are real but have no connection with the events in this book.

Cover Design by Charlotte Mouncey

Printed in Great Britain by Lightning Source UK Ltd

A CIP catalogue record for this book is available
from the British Library
ISBN 978-1-910077-80-1

Previous books by Colin Goodwin

Dont Get Mad, Get Even (Paperback)
ISBN: 978-1-910077-60-3

A rude awakening

'What the hell's happening?' he screamed inside his head.

Albert Bradley was very proud of the varnished tongue-and-groove panelling which clad the interior of his narrowboat, but not when his nose was pressed hard up against it. He was in total darkness, it was difficult to breathe and he could not shift himself from the corner of the bunk. It freaked him. He had been in that position for an hour or so, and he sensed that he was slowly slipping further and further into helplessness.

'Have I had a stroke?' he wondered, apparently in the grip of paralysis. He quickly twitched his fingers and toes. 'They seem OK,' he reassured himself.

Moments later, creaking and scraping noises from below robbed him of any self-control. Albert paused and tried to stifle his panic.

'Keep calm, keep calm,' he muttered, at the same time trying to breathe normally. He listened intently. 'It's gone quiet,' he thought. Then, just as he was about to raise his head, he heard a violent banging from just feet away in the galley. He wanted to breathe deeply, but he was afraid of giving away his location to whoever was obviously searching for something – and, in the process, trashing his boat.

Just as he thought all was quiet, the noise of another drawer being wrenched open and the contents being thrown to the floor stalled his breathing again. Panic set in. He clenched his fists hard, and could feel his long, grubby fingernails digging into the palms of his hands.

'What the frig are they after? There's nowt here but dirty washing and junk.'

The chemistry of sloppy mud meeting strong battery acid and old engine oil combined to create a musty, earthy stench that wafted in with the early morning mist and started to fill the cabin. Albert felt the cold vapour waft across his face. His mind raced and his nostrils twitched at the sour stink.

'The smell of death,' he whispered, his eyes wide at the thought. 'Is this it, then? How it will all end?'

He asked the question to the panelling.

'Will it hurt? Will it take long?'

He slid back under the duvet with just his eyes over the edge. He looked up at what appeared to be a shadowy shroud waving over his head and beckoning him. In fact it was the net curtains blowing in from an open window.

With his fists still clenched and eyes tight shut, he waited and waited … and waited.

Albert: A bit of history

Albert had only had the boat a year. This was because of the comings and goings in Throttle Village, a once-quiet village that was still reeling from the wrangling, the arson and the violent and tragic deaths associated with the now non-existent cricket club. He had been one of the lucky ones during its demise. As a result of the sale and development of the cricket ground, his house could now be sold at its appropriate market value, rather than the devalued amount it had previously been worth because of being so dangerously close to the outfield.

On the day that he stood in the kitchen and told his wife they had a buyer, he had not reckoned on other factors.

'We can relocate and move on. I've been down to the estate agent's and got all these brochures,' he told her in a forthright, domineering tone.

She stood in silence, staring at the wall and drumming her recently extended fingernails on the worktop. Then she turned to face him.

'Do you think so? Well, I'm afraid I've got other plans. I've had enough of you. I've been waiting until all this business with the cricket club and house was sorted. Well, now it is, and *I* am moving on, without *you*. We split the proceeds and go our separate ways. I am sorry, but that's how it is.'

'Bloody hell,' he stuttered.

She went on.

'Sorry, but I've had enough of your moods, your garden, the issues with the cricket club. You've been so engrossed you've not even noticed I'm here. So engrossed, in fact, that you've not noticed I've been knocking about with one of your old mates. As soon as the divorce comes through we're getting married then moving down south – where, apparently, it rains less and the sun shines now and again.'

'Divorce, divorce … not messing about, are you? The soddin' ink's not dry on the contracts. Anyway, which one?'

'See? You're not bothered, are you? Not bothered about the way you've treated me or, – should I say? – ignored me all this time.' She shrieked, raised a clenched fist and moved towards him. He backed away quickly and pulled a breakfast chair between them.

'Soddin' hell … I only want to know which one.'

'Yes, but you're not bothered… The way you've treated me… Not sorry, are you? Not sorry about us breaking up, are you? When was the last time you bought me flowers or took me out?' she shouted.

'Of course I'm sorry, love. Can we not talk it through?'

'Don't you ever call me "love" again. Communicate through the solicitor from now on.'

She rifled in her bag and produced a brown envelope, waved it at him, then threw it on the table.

'It's all in here,' she told him.

The front door slammed so hard it cracked the glass. Seconds later he peered through what was left of the pane and saw his now estranged wife climb into a van alongside her new partner. The sign on the van read,

Rubbish shifted. No job too small.
The irony was not totally lost on him. He tried to laugh, but the lump in his throat choked him. As he wiped away the tears he shouted, 'Come on … still got me sense of humour.'

***

So, with his half of the proceeds he bought a canal boat, a forty-footer: traditional narrowboat style. It had all mod cons: fridge, cooker, shower and solid-fuel stove.

'I can sail off into the sunset, meet new people and explore new horizons,' he would dream as he painted, polished and tinkered.

However, that is all he ever did: polish the brass, tinker with the engine, paint the hull and try to keep ahead of the rust. Even in the short term, the rust had started to beat him. One night when all was quiet he thought he could hear it creeping and crackling across the metalwork.

He had cruised left then right from his mooring for a day out, but had not reckoned on the anglers who verbally objected to him disrupting their lines – plus the kids throwing bricks from bridges – not to mention the dross he had to avoid while cruising. There was the time he fell in the water while manoeuvring in a lock. He went completely under, and recalled viewing the underside of his boat very calmly till he noticed that he was being drawn towards the thrashing propeller. In his mind he even saw the crimson water and pulped flesh as he bled to death. Fortunately his friend rescued him. He grabbed him by his mop of black hair and held him to the side until he could climb out.

The therapy of cruising turned out to be more

stressful than he could imagine. So that's as far as he got. The dream of sailing waned, and the boat became permanently and conveniently moored ten minutes' walk from the pub and five minutes from the chip shop.

However, today's circumstance was different. He felt paralysed and confused. He had spent most of the previous evening in The Old Anchor and recalled, 'Didn't have that many – maybe one to finish from the top shelf – so why can't I shift from the bunk?'

He shuddered as the words 'paralysis' and 'stroke' reappeared in his mind. In a split second he even visualised himself slumped in a wheelchair with a plastic tube in his mouth.

Another couple of hours passed before daylight revealed the reason for all the happenings. The canal had emptied and, as Albert's boat had settled on the canal bottom, it had tipped over to one side due to the sloping keel. All the drawers on the top side had slid open, fallen out and spilt their contents onto the floor.

When rescue came his mind had also slipped sideways. Lack of sleep and his vivid imagination had affected him. His once logical mind had departed, and his hair had turned a shade whiter. His usually laid-back demeanour was gone, to be replaced by that of someone who had spent the night with the Devil in a tumble dryer. Eventually he was helped out of his partially tipped-over boat by representatives from all three emergency services, who were in fact initially reluctant to offer any service at all. They just stared at the predicament and remained standing resolutely on the stone embankment. The paradox was not lost on the accumulating onlookers.

One pedestrian observed, then commented, 'There're more flashing lights than Blackpool Illuminations. All this gear and posh outfits, but no bugger's doing owt!'

To show willing, the 'rescuers' decided to test the firmness of the muddy bottom of the canal. They threw bricks high in the air and watched as they descended then submerged with a 'glup'. Mud splashed everywhere, ears pricked back, eyebrows raised and hands remained firmly in pockets.

'Jesus, that is deep,' said an ambulance man as he flicked mud off his uniform.

It was at this moment that Albert's face appeared behind the cabin window. He mouthed something incomprehensible, and the onlookers waved back.

They beckoned to him to climb from his boat to the bank, more in jest than in seriousness.

'Come on, it's not that deep,' they lied.

'Well, someone should go and help,' shouted a man out walking his dog who had stopped and was now reclining on the stone wall opposite.

'I'm stuffed if I'm going in … my outfit will be ruined. We have to buy these ourselves, you know,' added one helpful fireman.

'Besides, look at his face. He looks awfully sick,' he said as he pointed towards the ambulance man.

'We can put you a ladder across.'

The ambulance man looked up.

''Ave you seen his face? Criminal-looking – not ill, not sick – just criminal-looking, if you ask me.'

They all looked at the policeman, who at the time was reporting that all was well on his radio.

'On your bike … if you think I'm wading in that,' he replied, having witnessed the experiment with the bricks.

A crowd had gathered, attracted by the flashing blue lights. They stared at the dripping, weed-ridden hull, with its shiny propeller now out of the water. Then, as fish flapped their last in the shallow, muddy pools, a man clinging to the remains of his sanity and the sloping handle of a doorway ventured out.

'Are you not going to help me, you set of gits?' he screamed.

'Get a rope. Come on, we've got to get him out. I've got riots to attend to,' the policeman instructed the firemen.

'Jump, jump,' bayed the now swelling crowd.

The fireman threw one end of a rope, which landed on the back of the boat.

'Come on, grab the rope,' he shouted.

Albert crept towards it gingerly. Then, when he tried to stand up on the deck, which was at forty-five degrees, he slipped and slid unceremoniously off the back of the boat.

It was a soft landing, as predicted. What looked solid from the banking was in fact twelve inches of sloppy silt.

'See, I said it were deep,' announced a fireman with an element of 'I told you so'.

The emergency services nodded to each other, which confirmed the results of the experiments.

Meanwhile Albert had disappeared. The mud had covered him like a thick grey blanket. Then, with the whites of his eyes blinking, he rose up like a serpent from the deep. He had to be hauled out by a rope around his waist. The audience and the services roared with laughter as the unrecognisable Albert left a trail of mud towards the ambulance. It took him ages to recover.

A noise he had failed to hear amid the bellyaching laughter was the rapid whirr and click of the *Throttle Flyer*'s latest in a line of eager reporters, who captured every embarrassing moment. The hypothermia inflicted by the ambulance driver's insistence that he had to be gently hosed down by the firemen prior to being allowed in the ambulance meant a stay in hospital for a few days.

It was as he lay back in his sickbed that he received a copy of the local free paper. Emblazoned on the front page, a photo showed him covered in dark grey silt with just the whites of his eyes showing. The caption heading asked the question,

Loch Ness monster?

'You bastard,' he snarled, screwing up the paper. 'Well, we'll see about you.'

Location, location, location

The background

Throttle Village sat on the outskirts of the North York Moors. It had been an isolated, sleepy setting until a new link road provided easy access to Bradford or Leeds. Inevitably, Throttle became popular. The cheap and affordable stone-fronted terraced houses sold quickly, and prices were rising.

Two suited gents sitting at the back of the newly opened Italian café had not missed this profitable opportunity. They were relaxing in distressed leather seating that was surrounded by dark oak panels displaying images of rural Italy. Scraps of paper covered with calculations cluttered the small table. Finally one gent rattled the keys of an old calculator, then heavily underlined a six-figure sum. Other customers gave them only the slightest attention as they raised their coffee cups and toasted their situation.

'There's a killing to be had,' they said.

Their plan was to supply affordable houses for the workers, and executive-style houses for those who could afford it. The housing need for the area had become urgent, and so the two local entrepreneurs – or robbing bastards, as they were better known – set about to feed the need, and make a bundle in the process.

More recent history

Joe Lagg, estate agent, and Roland Bullock, landowner, both excelled at being able to do people a bad turn. Roland had successfully wrenched the land back from the cricket club, and had miraculously got planning permission for the houses. This was a pursuit which had afforded him a short period in prison on a charge of manslaughter, until an expensive barrister proved that there was no case to answer – though the detailed account of him running away from the scene minus his trousers had required an awkward explanation, and had meant that he had had to lie low for a while.

Joe Lagg, on the other hand, had made a career and a fair wage out of exaggerating the positives of a property and purposely hiding any negatives – a typical estate agent's tactic, he reassured himself.

And so two new housing developments had been instigated. One was aptly named Bullock Mill Estate after Sir Alfred Bullock, father of Roland and previous owner of the land it was built on. These houses, which were built on the brownfield site and located on the perimeter of Throttle Village, could – according to the architect – be, 'Community, three-storey, affordable houses'. However, on completion, the description soon became, 'Cramped town houses with sod all outside'.

With this type of property it was recommended that

you got on with your neighbour. In comparison to the traditional stone-fronted terrace, you were closer in proximity to the people you lived next door to, and there was less in the way of sound insulation … more like a commune than a community.

However, the site formerly occupied by Throttle Cricket Club – and nearing completion – was described in the glossy brochure as boasting, 'Houses of high status for today's family'. The houses were either semi-detached or detached, but what they had in common was that they created rivalry in the form of keeping up with the Joneses: a bigger or a better-kept garden, a conservatory added after moving in, a gravel drive or – if you had a semi – the desire to move up to a detached house.

Roland held court.

'We stoke the fire of greed by constantly offering a better place to live than the next person has.'

'You mean opportunity,' responded Joe, hoping he could appear to be part of the conversation.

'No, I mean they will always be slaves to our drum.'

Joe paused, and could only offer a witticism.

'It's a cymbal of the times we live in… Get it?'

'That's too much for one day. I'm off,' announced Roland, and waved to the waitress for the bill.

And so the two unskilled building developers set about the task of creating two massive housing estates with little more knowledge than your average DIY person. Their plan acknowledged this fact, and they reasoned that if there was a shortfall in ability then any skills they required could be bought in off the shelf, like a packet of screws.

Satisfied with this arrangement, and against their better judgment, they then had to decide on accomplices for this venture. They needed individuals with some building experience, plus the vital qualities of deference to them and a certain bouncer-type presence to protect them from any physical altercation.

Ideally suited to this job description were the Jakeson brothers. When approached by Roland to take charge, they were surprised to find that their job title took a great leap from being local jobbing builders to site managers overseeing a massive financial development. What could go wrong?

Hot and cold running…

Averill Jones, her teenage son Richard and her husband Gordon were driving towards their recently acquired 'high-status' house.

Previously they had lived in one of the many stone-fronted terraced houses that lined the village, but trouble with the neighbours about the noise they created had forced a move.

Richard had asked if he could play an instrument – a bass guitar, he suggested – to enable him to join in a group with his mates (but primarily because he had the notion that it made him more attractive to the opposite sex). His parents were keen to support this musical desire, but had differing thoughts about the choice of instrument. Educational expectations were high for Richard, and considered opinion suggested that the ability to play a more restrained classical instrument could get him into an improved higher educational establishment.

This did not impress Richard, who accused them of interfering in his desire to emulate his hard rock heroes. In an effort to pacify him and persuade him, his mother took him to see the locally revived brass band, and cajoled him into joining by saying it had girls from the area in its membership. In fact it only had one: shy Jane Summerbee, who could not believe her luck when Richard turned up for practice with his grandfather's old cornet.

'Your grandfather played it in the band, and he would have loved you to have it,' simpered his grandmother. 'Your dad wouldn't go near it,' she added bitterly. 'He was too busy messing with his motorbike.'

Unfortunately the practising had not gone down too well with the neighbours. Continually repeating the theme tune to *2001: A Space Odyssey* had driven the couple next door to breaking point – so much so that the usually calm and amicable gentleman had shouted through the dividing wall that he would, 'Shove it up the lad's arse blunt end first if he doesn't put a sock in it.'

In an effort to continue with this vital string to Richard's educational bow, the couple decided to find a property that would allow him to continue to practise without disturbing the neighbours, or that was the theory.

They had sold their house without any problems to a couple who, ironically, wanted to move out of the newly built community housing. Gordon felt strange when he was showing the couple round. They went into raptures about the large gardens, tall ceilings, stained-glass panelled doors and spacious rooms.

'Why are you moving?' they quizzed.

'Why are we moving?' he asked his wife after they left.

Unfortunately the prospect of a high-status house was too much for his side of the argument, so contracts were signed and exchanged and they were now in the process of getting the new house ready for moving into.

'I'm so excited … aren't you?' beamed Averill as she asked the question. 'Curtains, blinds, a three-piece suite, kitchen bits and bobs, dining room furniture, bathroom fittings… What a shame. Nothing fits in from our old house.' She turned to face him. 'Well, aren't you excited?'

Gordon, who had taken most of their belongings to the tip because they *just did not fit in*, gripped the steering wheel and bit his tongue as they drove to their new abode.

As they turned the corner into Outfield Avenue the conversation stopped, and the question become redundant. Instead they were confronted by workmen and other householders waving their arms – some shouting and some crying.

Gordon smiled.

'What could be this bad?' he tittered.

What he failed to see was the strangely coloured water seeping out from under the front doors and running down the drives. He parked the car, then stepped out into an inch of flowing water.

Moments later Gordon ranted, 'I want my money back right away. I knew this was a crap idea,' as he stood ankle-deep in the water that covered the newly laid carpets.

Meanwhile Averill ran from room to room screaming, 'There're fish in the kitchen, the sink's full of fish, the downstairs shower's full of fish. There're even fish in the toilet…' at which point she ran from the house, splashing through the dirty water, and joined the others, who were sobbing in the middle of the road.

At the rear of one of the houses a meeting of minds had begun. The contractors who installed the sewage pipes remained puzzled as they stared down the manhole in one of the gardens. They shone a torch and were amazed at what they saw.

'Fish … what on earth's going on here?' said one workman as he leant forward and gripped the edge of the manhole. He exhaled, flared his nostrils and took a deep breath. He then stood up, red-faced with the activity, and announced, 'It's not sewage. There's no shit in this. It's a more environmental odour, with a hint of mammal and subtle tones of amphibian,' he suggested, with the same authority as a wine expert.

The others grinned to themselves as they mocked his knowledge.

'It's my job: I'm paid to know these things,' he added with pride.

They laid out the diagram of all the sewage pipes, and traced with a muddy finger from the houses to the main sewage connection on the outskirts of the village. One of them stood on a ladder and visually traced the route of the underground sewer pipe.

'No ponds or anything, are there?' they queried.

'Nothin',' was the blunt reply.

'An act of God, then? Apparently he could make it rain with fish.'

They looked skywards for an answer.

Those in charge

In the site office the sense of humour was long gone. It was replaced with wide-eyed panic. The two Jakeson brothers, of Jakeson Homes Ltd (formerly Jakeson & Jakeson, builders and bodgers), were surveying the site map. Using a felt-tip marker held by a shaking hand, they placed a dot on each of the houses that had the water problem.

Reginald, the elder and saner of the brothers, assessed the situation.

'Seventy-three out of the 150 houses have got water gushing the wrong way up and out of the drains. Fish, weeds and all sorts are running down the drives.'

Simon, who always saw things from a different angle, offered an alternative insight.

'The design created by the felt-tip marker is triangular. It starts at the far end of the site and widens as it goes along. Spooky,' he said.

He reached into a cupboard and took out a well-thumbed manual.

'I can't understand it,' he added, hastily thumbing through *The Guide to Modern Plumbing*.

Reginald shook his head and watched as Simon ran his finger down the index.

'Nowt in here about fish in the system,' he confirmed.

'Have you looked under W for weeds, or F for frogs?'

On realising he was being mocked, Simon slammed the book shut. As he put the book back in the cupboard he glanced out of the window and caught sight of a group of residents marching towards them.

'Well, you'd better find some answers from somewhere. There's a bleeding lynch mob coming down the street.'

Reginald peered through the window, then dashed over and locked the door from the inside.

Simon grabbed hold of his chair and moved it against the door, then sat in it.

'Just a precaution,' he whispered.

'This'll ruin us,' predicted Reginald with gloom in his voice.

Simon put his hands to the side of his face and, in a ghostly voice, suggested another answer.

'It's like a plague, a plague of fish. It's a reckoning for our past sins.'

Reginald sighed.

'Just for confirmation – if you are getting biblical – it were frogs.'

***

Previously they had been just builders. They had no real knowledge apart from a couple of years on a night school course, and the rest they picked up as they went along. They relied mainly on brute force and lots of ignorance, but this venture was different. Architects, planners, building regulations, banks, solicitors and estate agents were also involved, and so most of the time they felt – and were – out of their depth. This administrative role was not to Simon's liking, and he frequently made it clear to his elder brother.

'I'd rather be knocking a wall down,' he would moan

as he stared at an increasingly large pile of mail in a cardboard box marked 'In'.

Their role in the venture meant that they were directly responsible to Joe Lagg, with whom they had a strained relationship. They were happy with his nominal support and he was happy with their compliance, and – when needed – their nightclub bouncer image.

They stared at the increasing mass of people outside the hut, then at the plan of the houses, then at the kettle.

'Best ring Joe. Put him in the picture first. Then we'll have a brew,' suggested Reginald.

Simon, whose major qualities were digging holes or making the tea, offered a philosophical observation.

'Is a bird in your bush better than a fish in your sink?'

Reginald was used to his absurd comments, and so retaliated.

'Is a phone in your ear better than a boot up your arse?'

Joe Lagg, or can things get any worse?

The project was also taking its toll on Joe. The houses were going up fast, faster than he could keep track of. He also was sinking under the endless administration relating to housing construction. Prior to this venture he had been just a local estate agent and, as such, the paperwork was minimal. Any paperwork that needed attending to was passed quickly to his secretary, and anything complex was passed over to the solicitor.

'What a job,' he would smirk as he toiled over the daily crossword.

More recently it was a different story. The endless meetings, deadlines and bureaucracy of the planning department were beginning to have an effect in the form of self-doubt.

His secretary could frequently hear him mutter through the half-open door, 'Far too complicated: not my idea of fun at all. What have I taken on here?'

He was looking in the mirror, and could swear he was looking older. He pulled at a recently acquired tuft of greying hair and wondered, 'Do I cut it off or colour it in?' He was also watching the lower eyelid on his right eye twitching uncontrollably. He tried steadying it with a finger, but the twitch returned the moment he moved his finger away.

He peered hard at his own reflection and noticed a

crease on his face.

'This wasn't here yesterday … and the dark rings? Stress, and sleep,' he muttered. 'Less stress, more sleep. Vicious circle, though. It's the frigging stress that's stopping me from sleeping … deadlines, cash flow going round and round in my head.

'It'll not be long now,' he consoled himself. He would close his eyes and imagine himself lying by the pool under a shade, holding a rum and Coke.

'The Canary Islands, red wine, hot sun, a cool pool and loads and loads of relaxing sleep,' he smiled. He tilted his head from side to side to audibly crack his neck joints, and then straightened his tie.

'Phone call, Mr Lagg,' shouted his overworked secretary.

'Who is it?' he replied, not moving from the mirror.

'It's the odd couple from the site,' she replied, holding her hand over the mouthpiece.

He picked up the phone in his office and listened. His face seemed to sag, as if affected by an increase in gravity. Within seconds his dreams began to crumble, and his eye twitched even more.

'No, no… We have sold those houses… They can't have their money back… You sort it… Don't succumb to threats… Look, we have a lot of money invested in this project… Do what you do best… Do what you're paid for… Beat them up if you have to… Just sort it, OK?'

His hand trembled and he dropped the phone.

'Fish in the bath, weeds in the toilets. What's going on?'

His secretary looked at him, and then offered a 'What did I say?' comment. 'Registered plumbers, were they?'

'How the hell should I know?' he replied angrily.

He staggered to a chart on the wall, which was identical to the one the Jakeson brothers had in their hut. He ran his finger along the line of houses, counting as he went.

'We're down to the last ten to sell, and 140 are sold… twenty million quid's worth… Now worthless… We've bills to pay… We should have known better… The soddin' Jakesons.'

He glanced in the mirror and blinked. Then both eyes twitched.

A long way away in sunny climes

On a marble-floored balcony looking out to sea Robin, who had just applied lashings of after-sun lotion to his red face, grinned as he listened intently to Large Richard on his mobile phone.

Then, obviously pleased, he replied, 'Great. Job's done, then... Er, no evidence ... you sure?' he said, with an element of suspicion.

'Na. Went like frigging clockwork,' came the gruff reply.

'Cheque's in the post, then. Catch you later, Dick.'

'Er ... cash, if you don't mind.'

'Yeah, no probs. I'll get it to you.'

Robin pressed the end call button, then mused for a moment before wiping the after-sun lotion from the keyboard. He employed Large Richard to attend to everyday jobs that required a person of a certain size – but as he usually delegated the jobs one at a time, he wondered how Large Richard would manage when he had to think for himself, because multitasking was not in his make-up. He had acquired the name Large Richard after a fellow builder on the construction site of a motorway bridge shortened his name and referred to him as 'Big Dick'. Rumour had it that the builder now formed part of one of the supporting pillars of a flyover.

In the hotel bathroom Robin attended to his

increasingly crispy face.

'I'll teach the bastards to mess me about,' he said to himself as he dabbed more cream on his inflamed nose.

On the other end of the line Large Richard smirked as he put his phone back in his pocket.

'Well, not much frigging evidence…'

Water, water, everywhere…

The police officer whose day had got off to a bad start received another call.

'What's going on? Did I hear you right? Go and rescue the Jakesons from their hut…? On my way.'

As he drove along he tried to work out what the commotion could be about, then burst out laughing at the prospect.

'Sounds like some of their chickens are coming home to roost.'

On arrival he noticed that the car was splashing through a stream of water, but took little notice of what it was or where it came from. He parked and opened the door, only to find that he had to wade through a torrent of running water. Unaware that the water was running from the driveways, he paddled towards the site hut, which was surrounded by irate householders – who by now had armed themselves with builders' tools and were waving them in the air.

'Never thought I'd see the day…' he laughed. 'The Jakesons being threatened. Usually it's the other way round.'

He observed the rush of dirty water and dead fish, and followed it to its source.

'Bleeding hell,' he gasped.

A house owner grabbed his arm.

'That's right: it's coming from my house,' he shouted.

The police officer made his way to the hut and squeezed through the mob.

'Now, if we can have some calm, I am sure the contractors are on to it … aren't you?' he said, looking sternly at the brothers, who were still in the hut. But they held up their hands and shrugged their shoulders.

Not satisfied with their response, the police officer asserted himself.

'I am sure they will fix it … won't you?' he said, loudly enough to rattle the window.

The brothers got the message and lowered their arms. Then they nodded excitedly, but with a sickly grin.

Men in yellow scratch their heads

The haste to solve the mystery of the canal dewatering got underway. The police informed the waterways department, who in turn delegated to the engineers located in the area. The objective was simple: find the leak. The selected men drove to the locks at the start of the now empty section of canal. They donned their high-visibility waterproof coats and watched from the stone bank. On one side of the lock the canal was empty. On the other side it was full of water.

'It should be simple enough,' they concurred.

As the water squirted through the gaps in the ageing lock gate they set off to walk the length of the dewatered canal. It was a pleasant stroll. The sun was shining and the birds were singing, but despite careful inspection they could find no breaches, nor a collapsed bank. They had both worked for the company for years, but had never experienced anything like this. After they had walked about a mile they started to have doubts about what had happened, and one of the engineers said, 'I can't understand it. It's usually dead obvious when summat like this happens. It's usually as a result of a storm or a massive downpour, when the banks can't cope with the extra water. Usually you see the problem right away.' He glanced at the calculator on his mobile phone. 'I've had a quick reckon-up: up to now it's 545,000,000 gallons.

Where's it all gone? The locks are sound. So are the banks.'

His colleague was a little less mathematical.

'It's not rained for a couple of days, and it has been hot,' he mumbled, looking skywards.

His partner refused to give the comment any credibility. From then on, they walked in silence, both struggling to find an answer. They reached another lock to find water on the other side – effectively, a full canal. They scratched their heads again, but this time a bit harder.

'We are going to have to walk back and this time look more carefully,' they said to each other.

***

Twilight was approaching as they came across a field much lower than the canal and, beyond the field, they could also make out the odd light and the outline of the new housing estate. A dark shape in the middle of the canal caught the eye of one of them.

'Bloody hell,' he gasped. 'Can you see it?'

'See what?' said the other man, screwing up his eyes.

'The hole, you blind git. The hole.'

They stood on the embankment facing the field, and in the diminishing daylight could just make out a dark shape snaking across the field. They clambered through the bracken down the embankment and stared into a neatly cut ditch stretching from under the canal and straight across the field to the other end, where the new housing estate was located.

As they followed the ditch across the field a crumpled heap caught their eyes. As they got closer it became obvious that it was not just a bundle of old clothes.

'Oh God, get the police,' said the man to his partner.

A roaring fire, alcohol, and a job well done?

On the outskirts of the town a pub usually devoid of customers on a weekday had a punter with a thirst. Most of the early evening drinkers had drifted away, but one customer in the Ramshackle Inn was mellowing nicely. Of a heavy build and wearing the statutory builder's boots and a torn waxed jacket, his ruddy appearance suggested that he spent many hours working in the fresh air with a bellyful of alcohol for insulation.

Large Richard had parked himself in front of the roaring coal fire and was savouring a pint of best bitter with a glass of malt whiskey as a chaser. The barman leant forward and whispered to a local, and at the same time nodded towards the fire.

'I asked him, "Is it a celebration?" You know, as I was using the optic – just a friendly comment – and then he said, "Sort of. Just mind your frigging nose." He meant it, too … real miserable, like.'

The barman pointed towards the trail of mud.

'Have you seen the mess? God knows where he has been.' He and the customer followed the trail of soil that had accompanied the man to the fireplace.

Just as Richard's head tilted back in the easy chair and he started to nod off, his phone rattled on the table.

'For frig's sake,' he muttered as he searched for the

button.

He listened a while, then spoke to the caller.

'Don't worry, it's taken care of... No witnesses... No frigger will think it's you. Just you make sure the cash is on its way.'

With that he put down the phone and turned to the barman. He did not speak. He just held up the glass and pointed to it.

'Friggin' witnesses,' he laughed.

A farmer's life is not a happy one…

The farmer whose field had had the trench dug across it also stared into the flames of an open fire with a glass of whiskey in his hand, though his whiskey was a little rougher. As he watched the flames, and the alcohol started to hit the spot, he began to ramble. He had suffered in the past few years. First, his wife had left him, though he had not blamed her.

'It's a rough life for a woman. Mind you, she knew what she was letting herself in for,' he consoled himself.

His ex-wife's parting shot, though, did not reflect his theory.

'If you think I'm working all the hours God sends, you can think again.'

Almost immediately after her leaving, his farm became infected with the mad cow disease that was raging across the country, and all his stock had to be slaughtered.

'Sheep, cattle, goats … shot the bleeding lot, and then burnt them in the top field. The whole area stank for weeks,' he shouted at the crackling flames.

He used the period after the killing of his animals to clean up the outbuilding and mend fences as instructed by the authorities, so that as soon as he got the all-clear he could start again. It was weeks until he could restock the farm. Then, just as he got going, it all happened again.

'TB, then after that bluetongue, and the new ones had

to be shot as well. Sod all will grow on that hill after all them bonfires.'

He poured himself another generous glass of whiskey and swallowed hard, as though he hated it.

His instructions from the man with the gruff voice had been simple:

'Do not get in touch, at any cost.'

'Hey, nobody mentioned fatalities,' he reasoned to the fireplace.

The farmer rummaged in an envelope for the number he was not supposed to use.

'What's the point in giving it to me if I'm not meant to use it?'

He put on his glasses and lifted them up slightly to aid his alcohol-soaked vision, then carefully pushed the tiny buttons.

***

In the pub the big man's phone rattled again. He had nodded off and did not hear it at first, but the customers did. As he awoke he felt their annoyance, and sneered back at them.

'What the hell's up with you?' he drawled. They shook their heads and looked away.

He read the digits on the display.

'Piss off,' he grunted.

He did not answer, just sneered and folded away the phone.

'You git,' muttered the farmer as he listened to the recorded message. 'Well, if you think I'm getting caught up in this…'

He put another shovel of coal on the fire and wondered about his circumstances. He considered himself an innocent bystander in this situation but, on the other hand, he knew that as soon as he had set eyes on Richard he should have known better. He should have known that he was a wrong 'un.

'I know what people will think, but I need the money. This place has not earned a bean for years. Sodding business plans from the bank, tax forms from the government, risk assessments from the health and safety, hazardous substance forms… Well, they can all piss off. Let them try and earn a living from this so-called green and pleasant land.'

He ruminated, took another swig of whiskey, grimaced, then opened his eyes wide as though he had seen a vision.

'But now survival is the name of the game,' he mused, while looking at the twelve-bore hooked on the ceiling beams. 'That'll need cleaning and oiling,' he continued.

He opened a cupboard drawer and took out a cardboard box. Inside were just three shiny new cartridges.

'So milk, tea bags and more of these,' he mumbled as he wetted the end of the pencil prior to writing a list.

Confusion at the angling club meeting

In a committee room at the local civic hall the well-attended monthly meeting of Throttle Angling Club was getting underway. After the usual reports the chairman addressed the assembly.

'Well, I'm flummoxed,' he said.

He held aloft a handful of printed leaflets that clearly advertised an event:

Fishing competition. Big prizes for the heaviest catch

'We've paid up front for these. We would use them again, but they've got the date on. It were all planned – the canal banks were all marked out, names were allocated to places – but how can you have an angling competition with no water? One day it was there. The next day it was gone. They haven't figured it out yet, but it's put paid to the competition.'

Most of the audience looked bewildered and shrugged their shoulders – apart from one young man, who kept his arms folded and his head down as he gripped a half pint of beer and concealed a smirk.

The chairman put down the leaflets and paused for a moment.

'But anyway, we have a more sombre announcement – and, to be honest, the competition pales into insignificance. Young John, a club member – a lad from down the road – was found dead yesterday in a muddy ditch up at Fossit's farm. That's all we know. The police aren't saying anything.'

The young man who was still clutching his glass choked on his beer and sat up. The others looked in his direction. There was a short silence as they allowed him to regain his composure. He coughed, cleared his throat then apologised.

'Sorry … he were a mate of mine. Sorry.'

Closing time

Richard sat in the armchair next to the fire, toasting the soles of his boots. He had succumbed to the soporific effect of fresh air and several alcoholic drinks and was now snoring loudly. Suddenly the clanging of the bell for last orders startled him, and he was not best pleased. He snarled at the barman, who had tentatively suggested it was time Richard went home.

'Sorry, it's the law. You know the licensing hours.'

He looked at the fading embers in the fireplace, then towards the barman.

'So you've taken my money. Now you want me to push off. Is that it?' He staggered to his feet and unsteadily made his way to the door. The barman stepped back from the edge of the bar. As Richard went past he tried to reason with him, but should have known better.

'It's going up for midnight, and we all have homes to go to.'

'Some of us,' Richard grunted as he kicked open the door.

He felt his way along the front of the pub, then went round the corner to the car park. As he stumbled towards his four-by-four a figure approached. He squinted as he caught site of the lad from the fishing club hiding in a doorway. Richard had had a long day and he was feeling tired and tetchy. The last thing he needed was an inquisition.

'What the frig do you want?' he groaned.

The lad, red-faced and distressed, moved out of the shadows and into the illumination from the security light of the pub.

'He's dead,' he bawled.

Richard raised his arms as if to say 'Tough'.

'"A hundred quid for an hour's work," you said. "All you have to do is crawl up this hole and poke around," you said. Well, he were my mate, and he's dead now,' the lad wailed out loud.

Richard looked up to the bedroom windows of the houses opposite the pub to see if the noise had raised anyone.

'He was unlucky. It were an accident,' added Richard as he moved forward.

'Well, you'll not get away with it. I'm off to the…'

Richard did not hesitate. A powerful right hook felled the lad, and then he repeatedly kicked him.

'No witnesses, Robin said there were to be no witnesses,' he drawled as he repeated his conversation with Robin.

He looked down at the lifeless body of the lad, grabbed him by his shirt collar and dragged him to a clump of bushes.

'Well, now there are none.'

Mid morning, Throttle Main Street

To Joe Lagg, mid morning always seemed to be a dead period, which was an unfortunate coincidence as he stared out from his estate agent's window. He studied the billboard outside the newsagent's across the street. The more he looked, the angrier he became. The board read:

Murderer sought in connection with doomed estate

'What are they on about? "Doomed estate", my arse. It's just a bit of damp … soon be sorted … all the business we put their way … adverts and such… They'll have us going bust with comments like that,' he muttered as he rummaged for the phone number.

As he dialled his rage increased until he was spitting out the words. His eyes bulged as he waited to be connected. Moments later he was speaking to the editor of the *Throttle Flyer*.

'Here I am trying to earn an honest living, and all you can say is "Doomed estate…" It's just a bit of damp.'

On the other end of the line the editor held the receiver away to avoid ear damage, and then spelt it out.

'OK. Let's see, then. *Estate agent plays down damage to homes, and the death of local boy.* Is that how you want it to read, Mr Lagg?'

There was a silence, then Joe slammed down the phone. The editor put down his phone calmly, looked out of the window and sneered, 'You are on the list, Mr Lagg.'

Must have taken ages

After the discovery of the large hole by the two canal engineers, the police had a quick look and decided there was nothing to be gained by delaying the restoration of the bank. Once the magnitude of the situation had set in, word spread rapidly and interested parties arrived to add their voice to the clamour.

A hastily arranged site meeting concurred that the illegal excavation should be repaired as soon as possible. A spokesperson for the businesses relying on the canal laid it on the line and stated, 'It's our busiest period. Already there are boats stuck on either side of the drained section. The boat hire people will go bust if we don't sort this out. Reputations are at stake here.'

Representatives of the waterways company nodded in unison, and gave the go-ahead to move in with heavy equipment.

On further inspection they found a partially concealed tunnel in a wooded area that went under the canal. From there a neatly cut ditch had been excavated in the field down towards the estate. This connected directly with the drainage system of the new estate. When the canal emptied it had funnelled water straight towards the new estate. The force of the water had been too much for the natural drainage system and, therefore, the canal water backed up into the houses.

This theory was being explained to onlookers to impress upon them the enormity of the task. Meanwhile two engineers hesitated at the still-dripping entrance to the tunnel. Powerful torches in hand, the two dayglo-clad men tentatively entered the tunnel under the canal, their voices echoing morbidly.

'Not sure about this. It could easily cave in, and then there would be two more to add to the list.'

'It'll be all right. Just don't touch the sides.'

'It's slippery. How can I not touch the sides?'

'All right. Just don't press hard, then.'

They shone the torches deep into the tunnel and marvelled at the scale of the operation.

'Good Jesus. It must have taken ages to dig this,' the first one to enter said.

They made their way in ankle-deep mud, holding hankies over their mouths to filter the stench, and to add to the ghastly situation, tree roots dangled and dripped on them as they fought their way further in.

'I'll have nightmares for weeks about this,' the second one said.

Then they both stopped and peered upwards through the cascade of canal water still running through the bottom of the canal. The contrast with the bright daylight made them squint and shield their eyes.

'So when you're digging upwards – you know, poking up, perhaps with a stick or summat, getting close to t'bottom of canal and all that water above you – how do you know when you're going to break through? Do you wait for the first drips? Is there a noise, or a creaking sound? At what precise moment do you get the hell out of there?'

'Maybe you don't know. Maybe you're just too stupid.'

A beach of a day

Far away from the carnage, one person was looking forward to a day of chilling out. Having just risen, and it being too late for breakfast, Robin ordered coffee from room service. In the meantime he dragged himself to the bathroom and put on his bathrobe. He stared in the mirror, then cleaned his teeth in an attempt to remove the acrid taste of a cigar he had smoked the night before in celebration of a job well done.

Still unsure about his sobriety, he decided on some fresh air. He opened the balcony door and ventured out. The moment he looked down from his tenth-floor balcony he felt wobbly. So, holding on to the rail for support, he stared out to sea and yawned.

As the previous night's red wine began to wear off he poured himself a black coffee from a cafetière and idly flicked over the pages of the UK newspaper he had ordered. Although he was on a 'Get away from all the crap' kind of break, he was always concerned that he might miss something. He half-heartedly expected a tiny column about a mysterious flood in an unknown village with perhaps a smaller headline of,

New Houses Destroyed by Mystery Flood

When he spotted the real headline he choked on his hot coffee.

Double Murder Connected to Unexplained Flooding?

As he read on he dropped the cup, and his face took on a look of horror.

'Richard! More like brain-dead Richard… "Get the money I'm owed," I said. "If it's an issue then cause a bit of chaos, put the frighteners on them," I also said,' he ranted as he paced up and down the coffee-soaked balcony.

Out of sight, out of mind

Coincidentally, Roland Bullock was also away from the centre of activity. He had gone on a short break to visit his father in London, or so he told everyone. As he looked out of the window of the train he imagined his country pile. He spotted large, detached houses as he passed through Cheshire, then later on through Oxford. He watched other passengers in the first-class carriage busily tapping away on their laptops,

'Can't be arsed,' he muttered as another large house caught his eye. 'It will not be long now,' he thought as he relaxed smugly in his first-class seat.

The waiter enquired if he was OK, and Roland nodded.

'Certainly am. What can go wrong now?'

In response, the waiter offered a bemused expression.

***

Back in Throttle the car park of the pub was cordoned off with police tape, and a tent had been erected over where the boy's body had been found. Later, at a press announcement, the police confirmed that a heavy-footed person had kicked the boy to death and that the body had ended up under a bush covered in mud – but, strangely, his shoes were clean.

In the press room the *Throttle Flyer* reporter decided to

push his luck, and delved a bit deeper.

'Do you have any leads? Is it connected to the canal drowning? And how many detectives are on the case?'

'No, possibly, and none of your business.'

'Come on … it's news. We don't often get news round here.'

One of the detectives conducting the conference nodded towards a colleague. Immediately a burly policeman stepped towards the reporter as he pressed his point. The reporter recoiled and pointed a camera at him.

'Want your picture in the paper, do you, for harassing the general public?'

As the policeman closed in, he whispered, 'Want the camera inserted in you, do you?'

A nondescript car approached the scene outside the pub. As it slewed to a halt two police officers guarding the area smirked to each other.

''Ave you seen…?' one said to the other.

Two men wearing police-issue mackintoshes got out of the car. As they turned, their coats spun out as if powered by a large, hidden fan.

''Kin' 'ell, it's Digger and Spade,' they said in unison.

Then one muttered, 'Batman and Robin.'

The press meeting finished and the local detectives retired to the makeshift office, where they were confronted by two officious-looking officers from outside the area.

'Hello, I'm Detective Inspector Digger and this is Sergeant Spade, and we've heard all the jokes. Tell us what you know.'

Costain family bliss?

Cooking odours and steam billowed from the open window of the cramped kitchen-dining room in one of the new community houses on Bullock Mill Estate. Around the tiny dining table the Costain family sat down to their evening meal.

'Seen this, Dad?'

'Can't exactly miss it,' said John, her dad.

'I told you not to bring it to the table,' her mother complained.

'Come on, then. What is it?'

The girl unclipped the latch on the wooden box, then took out a gleaming chrome and black microscope. After setting it up on the table she twiddled with the knob on the side that moved the lens up and down.

'We have to plug it in. It's got its own light. Whatever we find we put between these glass pieces then focus, using this knob.'

'Hey, that's brilliant,' her father enthused.

'We have to look at everyday objects under the microscope, then sketch what we find.'

'Like flies' legs?' added her mother, trying to join in.

'No, it's more about the environment we live in. We have a list. See: water, dust, soil, sink waste…' she went on.

Her mother folded her arms in defensive mode.

'This is a clean house,' she said. 'I spend most of the day cleaning up after you two. You'll find no muck here.'

'We're not looking for muck. We are looking for environmental waste: bacteria, bugs an' such.'

'Bugs? We don't have any bugs in here,' her mother yelled.

'Then there's only one way to find out,' challenged her dad.

'After tea you get sorted, and I'll get the samples,' he said, grinning.

'Well, I think they've got a nerve. You'll get no samples from me,' said her mother.

Father and daughter looked at one another. Each pulled a face, then looked back at Mum and said, 'No thanks.'

Later, as they worked their way through the list of samples, the fascination with the topic increased.

'Hey, have you seen the size of the fleas the cat's got?'

Mother spilt her tea.

'Only joking,' her daughter laughed.

Afterwards her father flicked through the folder containing the sketches. He paused at one that looked like a scene from a Christmas card.

'Are you sure this is right?' he queried.

She turned and gave him a look that he recognised from her mother.

'I've sketched what I've seen, whether it's right or not,' she replied haughtily.

'OK, OK… It's just that I didn't expect to see snow in a soil sample.'

The enthusiasm for the activity faded from his voice as suspicion grew as to what it might be.

'Come on, it's bedtime. I'll help you put it away.'

As he lay in bed John was staring at the ceiling trying to recall details about the area from way back when.

'It was only a cotton mill … wasn't it?' The question kept him awake most of the night.

The following morning, jaded and tired, John sat quietly as he reflected on the situation at the breakfast table. The night had not given him any answers, only suspicions. Unaware of his dilemma, his wife carried on as usual, putting her daughter's lunch box together. Then she noticed his posture.

'Are you ill?'

'No, no. I'm OK.'

'Your tea's gone cold, and you're not eating your toast. Are you sure you're OK?'

'Yeah, sorry … didn't sleep that well.'

He helped with the microscope, then watched his daughter put the finishing touches to her homework.

'I think you will do very well today,' he added with less enthusiasm than he meant.

***

On his way to work he furtively stepped out of the front door, closed it behind him and looked round to make sure no one was around. He then quickly stooped, grabbed a handful of soil from the front garden and quickly shoved it into a sandwich bag he had taken from the kitchen drawer. He wiped his hands on the back of his trousers and regained his usual casual stride as he walked to work. He worked at a factory on the outskirts of the village that manufactured soap products. After clocking in at the warehouse he sneaked round the back of the factory to the research area. He waited near the staff toilet until a friend who worked in that department walked by.

'Gary, how are you doing?'

'OK till you turned up. What are you after?'

'Don't be like that, but I do need a favour. Stick this under your microscope and tell me what it is, will you?'

'I can't. It's against company policy. They're really tough about people doing jobs on the side. What is it?' he added as he peered into the bag.

'I don't know. That's why I've brought it to you.'

'You'll get me bleeding sacked if I get caught doing this.'

'Will a pint settle your nerves?'

'Two, more like— oh, and you will support me, my wife and my kids if I get caught.'

'But of course,' John replied as he handed over the small bag.

***

Later the same day he got an answer he had been half expecting.

'Best garden centre compost mixed with flecks of asbestos. Not a big percentage, but it *is* the nasty kind. Where's the sample from?'

'Sorry, can't say. Look … I really appreciate what you've done. I do owe you a pint or two, but I can't say.'

'Don't drop yourself in it. If it's a public building you are legally obliged to say. The environmental people are really keen on the proper disposal of this stuff. You can't just take it to the tip … all hell would break loose if you turned up with this.'

John scratched his head as he considered his next move.

'It isn't a public building – well, not quite – but thanks for the advice.'

'You'd better have this back. I don't really like handling the stuff,' added his mate as he held out the plastic bag. 'Don't take it home, and don't dump it.'

'So what am I supposed to do with it?'

His friend's shoulders sloped, and then he gave him some advice tinged with a caution.

'Probably go and see a health and safety expert, then a solicitor, and then the environmental agency, who will not thank you for messing about with this stuff. But whatever you do, you do not mention you brought it here, or that you gave it to me. Do I make myself clear?'

'Very,' John replied as he shoved the bag into his pocket.

Digger and Spade on the case

The services of the two detectives were usually needed when a case required good old-fashioned police work. Typically this meant some combination of canvassing, interviews, surveillance, security camera reviews and painstaking trolling through rubbish and other measures. They were not interested in forensic evidence or anything that meant using a computer. They relied heavily on intuition and gut feeling. Tapping the sides of their noses to indicate a hunch had become a mannerism much mimicked by their fellow detectives. Colleagues described them as throwbacks from the sixties – with screeching tyres, loud voices, and grabbing their hats and coats and racing out of the offices making comments like, 'Follow that car.'

The bosses could not wait for them to retire. They were an embarrassment to the force.

When their superiors found that the case located in Throttle involved two straightforward murders, and a chance for them to get their hands dirty, they were the automatic choice for solving the mystery.

'So what have we got, Spade?'

Spade flicked over his police-issue notepad.

'Two deceased, sir. One drowned in suspicious circumstances. The other died from internal injuries inflicted by what appears to have been a severe kicking.

We also have a mysterious canal dewatering that seems to be connected to both incidents.'

'Anybody see it happen?'

'According to one witness it happened in the early hours. We've not got much more out of him, though. The whole episode seems to have affected his sanity. His boat tipped over. Took his brains with it, according to the hospital.'

'All this happens and nobody sees anything?'

DI Digger had always wanted to solve a major crime – and even though the crimes that he was allocated were usually straightforward he could, without effort, blow them out of proportion.

He looked at Spade with scepticism.

'Seems to me we have one of those situations where people are afraid to assist the police in case there are repercussions. Notice any strange people knocking about?'

'This is Throttle, sir… They are all strange in Throttle.'

'You know what I mean. Any weirdos?'

'Apparently they think we are weird,' he said, looking at the coat rack.

'So … this dewatering, as you call it… What happened there?'

'The canal emptied. That water went down a recently dug, man-made channel … the canal is high up there. Whoever it was dug the ditch right past Fossit's farm, straight down to the new housing estate. Caused havoc … new houses ruined.'

'OK, go on. I am getting a picture here.'

He looked at the ceiling and stroked his chin.

'Two dead, flooded houses… Sinister goings-on here – I know it.'

Like a gypsy fortune-teller staring into a crystal ball, Digger stared at the single light bulb in the centre of the sparsely decorated room. He screwed up his eyes then, alarmingly, opened them wide.

'There's a grudge here. I can feel it.'

'Seems a bit extreme. A double murder, just because someone's got a grudge?'

'Ah, but there is a connection. Mud.'

Spade was used to his peculiarities.

'"Mud," you say… OK.'

'Yes, mud. Mud at the scene of both murders, mud at the housing estate … and presumably mud up at Fossit's farm. That's it. We have to start somewhere. What about this farmer? Was he not tending his flock as the massive machine dug the ditch? He must have seen it.'

'Says he was at his sister's.'

'Farmers don't go away. They live on the land. He's pulling your leg. Come on, up to Fossit's farm. He must have seen something.'

***

They grabbed their free-issue overcoats and hurried out of the office. Having clambered into the car they set off, burning rubber as they exited the car park. Other officers watched through the windows and sniggered. Moments later they headed up the country lane towards the farm, then pulled over in a gate hole. They leant over a dry-stone wall and their eyes followed the dark trench from the canal down towards the new housing estate.

'Do all this, and nobody sees anything? Never,' said Digger.

As they continued on up towards the farm the road changed to an unmade track with pothole after pothole.

'I bet there is a scrapyard at the end of this,' Spade joked.

Finally, they parked the car on the other side of a five-bar gate that marked the border of the farmyard. They could see the front door, but a sea of manure blocked their path.

'Farmers and shit: inseparable,' Spade said.

They lifted their trousers, tiptoed round the perimeter and eventually made it to the front door.

'Just look at my shoes,' Digger moaned as he hammered on the door.

Eventually the door creaked open just far enough to allow common courtesy.

'What the frig do you want?' barked Fossit the farmer.

Spade looked down at his shoes and offered a practical observation.

'Just getting us out of this shit would be a good start.'

He looked back at the part-opened door and asserted his official posture.

'This is DI Digger and Sergeant Spade. We are investigating the happenings in Throttle, and we would like a chat.'

They kicked their shoes against the door frame to remove the excess manure and followed Fossit into the farmhouse. As they walked in they looked around, sniffed the odour and frowned. They sat around a table covered with used crockery.

'Would you like a cup of tea?' Graham Fossit offered.

Spade looked at the unwashed cups and plates and sniffed the air again.

'We'll pass on that, if you don't mind,' he replied as he got out his notebook. 'So what happened?'

'This bloke asked me if he could practise with his

digger… Gave me a grand. How could I refuse? What did you say your names were?' asked Fossit.

'Digger and Spade.'

'I love coincidences,' smiled Fossit.

'Come on, get on with it. We haven't got all day. What do you know?'

'OK, keep your hair on. He said he wanted to practise digging a trench. Said he'd fill it all in after. He hasn't. Said that he wasn't up to much and he needed the practice, and that he didn't want anyone to watch. Said he was embarrassed. Didn't look the type to be embarrassed… Gave me a grand. How could I refuse?'

'So you say,' said Digger.

'What else could I do?'

Digger looked down at his shoes and wiped them sideways on the carpet.

'You could put all this shit in the trench,' muttered Spade as he looked down at his own stained shoes.

'What?' replied the farmer, oblivious to the comment.

'What did he look like?'

'Who?'

'The man who dug the ditch. Don't mess us about.'

'Oh, him. Bleeding enormous, and rough, but he drove a posh Merc. Just like a tractor, it was. He were dead insistent that I weren't around. Said if I was I could kiss goodbye to the money.'

'Anything odd about him? Scars? Did he have a beard, or anything?'

'No, but he was dripping in gold: rings, watch, necklace, bracelet … everywhere, even teeth.'

'Did he give you a name, a number or anything?'

'No.'

'So let's get this straight. A stranger comes up to you

and says if you let him dig up your field he will give you a grand, no questions asked, and says, "Oh, by the way, I don't want you around while I'm at it."'

''Bout the size of it.'

'So where did you go?'

'Went to my sister's. Ask her, if you like. Stopped two days. He'd packed up and gone by the time I got back, apart from the bleeding ditch, that is. It'll take me ages to sort that out.'

'You can always borrow a digger. We'll let ourselves out,' Spade laughed.

***

In the doorway, Spade offered another observation while trying to find a route back to the car.

'Have you noticed there's not an animal in sight, and yet this place is still full of shit. How can that be?'

'He has a phantom muck spreader and, if you ask me, he is full of shit too.'

Outside in the car they perused the scribbled notes. Spade dictated.

'So: big bloke, full of money, no questions asked... Here today, gone the day after.'

'Practising digging, my arse,' Digger replied, indicating that he didn't believe that this was the truth.

'No thanks,' laughed Spade. 'But there is that mud connection,' he added.

'He's lying through his back teeth.'

'Where there's muck there's brass,' added Spade.

'Cut it out. Just drive,' said Digger as the car's wheels spun in the mud.

'Where to?'

Digger sniffed the air in the car and looked down at

his shoes.

'The car wash, then a change of shoes.'

The homework pays off

After school Sarah Costain sat at the kitchen table and guzzled a glass of milk.

'How did you go on?' said her dad as soon as he got home from work.

'Yeah ... did right good. They put the pictures up on the wall. Got good marks ... hey, there's some houses round here that are full of bugs. Gary Wilkes in our class found bugs in the bed. His mum went mad.'

'And now the entire street knows,' said her mum.

'You've done well. Brilliant, in fact,' he added, though his mind was elsewhere.

'I need answers,' he grumbled as he put his jacket back on.

'Where are you going?'

'Just to see an old mate ... run a problem by him ... quick pint. I'll not be long.'

'What about tea? It's about to be put out. It'll not keep.'

His mind whizzed, and he missed the last question. He stepped out of the house, paused and looked down at the front garden.

'Can't believe it,' he muttered as he recalled his wife kneeling in the garden pulling out weeds with her bare hands. He pressed on and walked to the canal towpath. He had heard that an old school friend was living rough on a canal boat just outside the village, and from the articles in the local press it seemed he might have the certain skills to help. He stood on the stone edging and gazed into the drained section. He had never seen the bottom of a canal before. The amount of scrap iron sticking out of the silt fascinated him.

'That's shallow. It's just a muddy ditch full of rubbish,' he thought, amazed at how little depth there was. He became aware of the smell of rotting vegetation from the canal bottom and put his hand over his mouth.

'How do they live in this?' he muttered through a cough.

He continued along to where an old lock gate was doing its best to hold back tons of water in the upper section. The pressure was too much for the ill-maintained joints and hinges, so water squirted through the gaps in torrents.

Further on, in the fully watered section, old narrowboats were moored nose to tail and some side by side, with thick ropes holding them to the stone embankment. From a distance they all looked empty and derelict, but in the dim light of early evening, narrow shafts of yellowy light came from part-closed curtains while black smoke oozed from sooty chimneys. As he walked on he had to avoid the accumulated rubbish of everyday living on the canal: old bikes, odd lengths of wood and rolls of tarpaulin.

'It's like a rubbish tip,' he mumbled to himself as he searched for a familiar name on the sides of the boats.

Then he spotted the one he was looking for. 'Rising Sun' was written in canal script, with a painting of a glowing sun optimistically directing rays all around.

'Fat chance,' he said to himself as he knocked on the steel hull.

The sudden rocking of the boat indicated that the occupant was on his way. He stood back, as he was unsure if he had the correct boat or not. He heard the various latches being released. Then the door opened. He blinked as the occupier stepped onto the steel decking. He smiled as he recognised the adult features of an old school friend.

'Well, well… Never expected to see you again,' said Robert, the boat's owner, as he brushed his dreadlocks to one side and held out a hand. 'Come on board. Do you fancy a brew? It has been ages.'

Hesitantly John climbed on board the rocking boat.

'You get used to it,' added Robert as he saw John reach for a place to hold on to.

Once in the lounge area they sat opposite each other in comfortable leather-backed chairs. John rubbed his hands up and down the black leather arms of the chair.

'Very nice. I approve of this … better than our house.'

Robert tilted his head appreciatively. He agreed with the comment as he handed John a mug of tea.

'I like it,' he said.

John felt the need to converse with Robert prior to asking him a favour. 'It's less mercenary,' he thought.

'What's going on with the canal? I've never seen it drained like this. Are they doing a repair?'

'Not exactly a repair, although they now have to put right the damage to the canal bottom after someone put a hole in it and emptied it.'

'Someone emptied it?' John repeated back in amazement.

'Yeah … seems unbelievable. Millions of gallons gone, stranded boats … the only bit of good luck was that I am moored on this side of the locks, or else this boat would be sitting on the bottom.'

'How did they do it?'

'Whoever it was dug a hole under the canal and just let it all run down the hill. They flooded that new housing estate, and killed a lad in the process.'

They sat in silence for a moment, then John plucked up the courage to raise the subject of the front garden.

'I've got this problem. I was wondering if you could help.'

Robert sat forward on his chair.

'If I can,' he said.

John told Robert about the suspected asbestos contamination of the soil and related what the man at work had said.

'It's good advice,' said Robert. 'You don't want to be messing about unprotected with that stuff.'

'I was wondering if you could help find out how it got there, the history of the estate – you know, before it was built on … only you seem to have contacts, from what I've heard.'

'What have you heard?'

'Oh, nothing nasty. It's just that when anything crops up in the paper about planning or disputes and such, your name appears. You seem to be good at it … it's just a favour. That's all.'

'Not a problem. The houses haven't been up long, so there should be no difficulty in getting the info we need.'

'Thanks… Look, I know it seems ungrateful … but I've got to go, or she will smell a rat.'

'Ah, the obligations of married life. Someone's got to do it,' he said as he led him to the door.

'Surprised you're not hitched up. As I remember, you never seemed to be without.'

'That's kind of you to say so, but not many women can hack the confines of a narrowboat.'

John clambered onto the bank and waved. A sense of envy crept through him as he watched Robert close the door.

'Got to be a downside to living on here,' he thought as he set off back in almost total darkness.

A trouble shared?

Joe Lagg sat staring miserably at a flat pint of beer. The barman cleaned the surface of the bar up to the edge of Joe's pint then interjected.

'What's up with you? You've been staring at that for ages.'

Joe turned and looked up. His mouth opened, then closed. His brain rummaged for an informative statement but failed, so he didn't bother.

'Just a bad day, that's all.'

'Thought you were becoming like that grumpy git we had in the other night.'

'What grumpy git?' Joe sighed.

'Bloke in the other night bit me head off. I was only trying to be sociable. Full of shit he was, physically and mentally. Trailed it all over the place. Took me ages to clean up, and do you know what?'

'What?'

'I reckon he's the murderer ... you could see it in his eyes...'

As the barman prattled on Joe switched off to him. His mind was full of bankruptcy, ruin and sickness.

'Oh, God, no,' he spluttered as he held his hand over his mouth. He gripped the rail of the bar. His cheeks bulged and his eyes watered as he heaved, then brought back the previous pint. In an attempt to avoid vomiting on himself, he swivelled his head round and directed the contents of his stomach over the clean floor and the trousers of the barman. The pub quickly emptied.

He cleaned himself up in the toilets as best he could, wandered back into the bar, held out his arms and apologised to the barman.

'Sorry ... very sorry.'

The barman refused to reply, so he wandered home. He opened the front door of the darkened house and sighed. Everything seemed cold and dead. He sat on the settee and stared at the ceiling. After cleaning his mouth and regaining his composure he reflected on his predicament.

'No choice,' he thought as he picked up his phone. He scrolled through the names until he reached 'Roland Bullock'.

'He won't like it, but what the heck,' he said as he dialled. His index finger physically shook as he aimed it towards the call button.

'Hello, Roland. Is that you? Are you enjoying yourself?'

There was a pause as Roland recognised the number and the voice.

'Oh, it's you. And who else would you expect to answer my phone? Come on, cut the crap. What's up? You never ring unless there's a problem.'

'I don't know where to start.'

'Try the beginning.'

'Well, first of all the canal emptied. Loads of boats went to the bottom. It all went down a big hole ... unbelievable. It ended up flooding all our houses – well, most of them. Then they found a drowned body in the field that had the ditch cut across it. Then another body was found in the pub car park, though nowt to do with us—' At this point Joe took a deep breath.

'Well, now the people whose houses were soaked want their money back and… Well … it looks suspicious, but we don't know who did it.'

'Did what?' said Roland.

'Dug a trench straight for our houses. It was done on purpose. Somebody has a grudge, and we'll all go bankrupt,' he yelled.

There was another pause as Roland's mind tried to rationalise Joe's high-speed rambling.

'Nothing trivial, then?' Roland quietly muttered. 'So let's get this right: some bastard wants us broke, and is prepared to do double murder to achieve it. Good job I'm out of the way. Make sure you lock your frigging door tonight, won't you?' There was another silence as he deliberated. Joe looked at his phone, then shook it.

'There's nothing for it. Get the Blues Brothers on to it. Right up their street, this. Number one priority. Kick the shit out of somebody – everybody – till they get some answers. Anyway, I'm stopping up or down here out of the way… Be in touch. Bye.'

Joe stared at the phone as it displayed *call ended*, and wondered if he had actually got an answer.

'Did he respond to my plight, my hour of need? I called him for moral support. Did I get any? Did I hell. So here I am again, piggy in the soddin' middle. He's legged it down south and I'm left in charge with only Laurel and Hardy for company. Never mind: a trouble shared is a trouble trebled,' he mumbled as he ran down his mobile phone list for Reginald Jakeson.

'They should be in now watching children's TV,' he said sarcastically as he waited for a reply.

'Hello, Reginald. It's me, Joe. I need to pass a hot

potato on to you, courtesy of our leader.'

Reginald stood up from his chair and mouthed to Simon, 'It's Joe. Turn it off.' To aid communication he pointed to the television and twiddled his fingers.

Joe continued, 'The issue of the water and the drowning – or, should I say, who did it, and why – has been passed down to your good selves for investigation. Good old Mr Bullock, our leader, says you are ideally suited to finding out who did it – your credentials being the ability to inflict grievous bodily harm to anyone who gets in your way or refuses to cooperate. So off you go. Go and get some answers before we all go down the pan.'

'Will do. Over and out,' replied Reginald.

'Oh dear,' Joe sighed.

He went into the kitchen and put on the kettle. As he watched it boil he reflected on the conversation.

'I am an estate agent, not a mafia boss or anything. Did I really tell them to go and beat up a person I have never met? What on earth is happening?'

Simon, who had been listening in to the conversation, beamed and put his arms up in the air in celebration.

'Brilliant. Finally a proper job,' he shouted.

'He says he is going to pay us in spuds – weird,' added Reginald.

Robert plus dreadlocks plus information

Just after the evening meal, John Costain was watching meaningless television, although his mind was elsewhere, when his wife walked in from the kitchen.

'Here, your phone's just gone off … at least, I think it was your phone … strange noise from your jacket.' She held his jacket towards him.

He rose casually from his chair, took out the phone and read the display, which said, *Fancy a beer? Rising Sun. Robert.*

He dropped the phone back into his inside pocket and handed her the TV remote control.

'Sorry, love. Got to dash out. Won't be long.'

'Who is it? What's happening?'

'Look … I'll tell you later.'

He grabbed his jacket and hurried through the door. His wife stared at the closed door and wondered about the contents of the text.

'I'll find out later … perhaps when he's asleep,' she smiled confidently.

John arrived at the canal bank in no time. He ignored the debris and the other vessels this time, and went straight to Robert's boat. He tapped on the metal roof, and moments later Robert opened the door.

'Come on in. Don't mind the mess.'

'No probs,' said John as he strode over a bucket of logs.

They sat down facing a roaring fire.

'This is all right,' John added as he warmed the palms of his hands.

Robert said, 'I've got the information you wanted. The mill used to be owned by the Bullock family. Apparently they converted the mill into units after the cotton trade collapsed. One unit was into the manufacture of asbestos components. Rumour has it that they had to stop because of the dust and the waste ... problems with disposal.'

'I think I know where they put it,' said John, heaving a sigh.

'So what's the next move?' asked Robert as he held out two bottles of lager.

'Not sure. I was hoping you would have some answers. You see, if it got made public that our house is contaminated, we'd lose everything. If we kept it quiet and moved on, I'm not sure I could live with myself, besides it being illegal. I'd always wonder about the poor sods who moved in.'

'And if you stay, there's a good chance you'll catch something nasty.'

Robert went on, 'You have choices, but not many. First things first: get rid of the top layer of soil, then pave it over. Unfortunately it will keep coming to the top, but you can stall it in the short term. Bring the bags of soil here, and I'll get rid of them for you. If you go to the tip they will ask all sorts of questions. It'll get official, then the proverbial cat will be out of the bag.'

'That's a lot of soil ... and the plants?'

'The plants are OK. Just replace the soil. I've got loads of bags... Take your time, and do it in stages. That way there's less chance of being noticed.'

'She won't like it,' he said, referring to his wife.

'That's your problem, I'm afraid. On the other hand … if she's in on it then it won't matter, will it? Spell it out.'

'Not sure. It won't be easy. She's dreamt of this house for ages; now it's a nightmare.'

'Talking of nightmares, here you go.' Robert handed John two black plastic bags. He opened the first.

'Blimey,' he said as he pulled out a white boiler suit with a hood, rubber gloves and a dust mask. 'It's not exactly Christmas.'

'It's a must if you're shifting this stuff. You don't want to breathe it in, or touch it. Bag the lot, and bring it with the soil.'

'And the other bag?' questioned John.

'It's just full of more plastic bags.'

John got anxious. 'Oh, and how do you expect me to wear this and not cause a fuss? It might as well say "Toxic waste removal" on the back.'

Robert tilted his head. 'You do what you have to do, especially in the dead of night. First sort the soil, and then we sort out the bloke who sold it to you,' he said with feeling.

'Now you're talking, but I must go or I'll be in it up to my neck.'

'This wife of yours … wears the trousers, does she?'

'Don't go there.'

'Don't worry. I won't.'

The alternative detective agency

After being summoned by Joe Lagg, the two Jakesons decided that – although their expertise was in inflicting physical harm to those who disagreed with them – it might actually be a good first move to find out the identity of the individual. Then they could use their skills to better effect. So: detectives first, and thugs second.

'What do you think?' said Simon as he paraded in a white raincoat with the collar turned up.

'Well, if you want an honest answer, more sex pest than detective. Where's it from?'

'The charity shop. They've got loads.'

'There's a clue there. I'll stick to my donkey jacket, if you don't mind.'

'More navvy than copper,' retaliated Simon.

They stood and looked at each other.

'Contrasting, wouldn't you say?'

Reginald then asked a question. 'Why have we got a glazed back door in the middle of the office?'

Simon tapped his nose.

'It's not a door. It's an investigation progress board. We stick pictures on the glass and write on it in felt pen – the suspects, clues and such – like they do on the box.'

'It's a bit awkward, though. You've chosen a four-pane door.'

'It were the only one left.'

'OK. We'll work round that. So at the moment it's blank. Where do we start?'

Simon held up a felt pen.

'Go on, then. Who are the suspects?' asked Reginald.

'Not sure. Looks like we are going to have to kick the shit out of somebody to get started.' He rubbed his hands together. 'Just like the old days.'

Simon put the top on the felt pen, fastened up his coat and beamed.

***

Fossit the farmer had just settled down with a cup of tea in his favourite and only armchair. He was mulling over the questions from the police visit when a knock at the front door startled him. Not knowing who it was, he paused, but suspected it might be the burly builder.

'The bastard could have been watching … waiting for the police to go so he could harass me about the questions they asked,' he mumbled.

He peeped through the letterbox. He could see two sets of legs, and one white coat and one black coat.

'Weird,' he thought. 'I'm not buying anything,' he shouted.

'We're not selling anything,' said Simon.

Fossit opened the door gingerly.

'What the bleeding hell?' he said.

Simon and Reginald stood motionless. He pointed at them and started laughing.

'Good God, what are you dressed like that for?'

Simon moved towards him with clenched fists.

'Hold back,' said Reginald. 'We are S & R Private Investigators,' he said with purpose in his voice.

'S & R? More like S & M with that gear on,' sniggered

Fossit.

'What did I say about your white coat? Anyway, kill him,' Reginald hissed at Simon.

Simon gripped the farmer by his shirt and chest hair, and pushed him back against the door.

'We are making enquiries, and would appreciate your cooperation.'

'OK, OK,' he croaked as Simon squeezed his throat.

Reginald smiled. 'We really would.'

'OK, OK. What is it?'

'That's better. No more jokes, just cooperation. Now get in.'

They bundled the farmer into his house and pushed him through the hall and into the lounge. Simon looked around, then nodded towards the easy chair. He pushed the farmer backwards, and then towered over him.

'Are you sitting comfortably? Then I'll frigging begin... Daphne Oxenford,' Simon told the farmer.

Reginald turned to him. 'Stop it! This is serious business. Stop coming out with daft remarks.'

'*Listen with Mother*. I remember it. It were on the radio.'

'It was,' confirmed the farmer.

Reginald turned to the farmer.

'I – that is, we – need to know the name of the bloke who dug the ditch, or I set this idiot on you.'

At this point Simon offered a well-rehearsed snarl for effect.

'And, as you can see, he is such an idiot that he won't know when to stop. There will be blood and snot everywhere, and we would probably have to bury you in a shallow grave on your own farm with a shit topping so it looks like the rest of this place.'

There was a moment's silence as Fossit assessed his position. Simon, eager as ever, moved in.

'I don't know … just like I told the police.'

'Five minutes should do it,' said Reginald calmly. 'But only five, remember. Any longer and we'll have a messy corpse on our hands. We don't really want that.'

Simon smiled at the farmer.

'Five will be plenty.'

'For God's sake, I don't know,' the farmer said.

Simon rolled up the sleeves of his white coat.

'He were called Richard. That's all I know,' said Fossit. 'When he answered the phone he said, "Richard here".' The farmer halted his confession and added a strange smirk to his face.

'But if you really want to find him … he goes under the nickname Big Dick.'

'I see. So you want me to go around asking if anyone has seen Big Dick. You'll get me locked up,' added Simon.

Reginald smiled again and said, 'Ah … so you have his phone number.'

'He will kill me if I give it to you.'

'And we will do worse than kill you if you don't.'

Simon passed him a pen and pad.

'In your best handwriting, if you please.'

Best served cold…

Albert Bradley had plenty of time to think, and he had plenty to think about. So he made a list, then highlighted the priorities. First, on the basis that he no longer had a place to live, was the righting of his boat after the canal draining. He had been back to look at it from the embankment, along with several other gongoozlers. It had become an attraction: there were people pointing at the almost upturned hull, and families picnicking in the field opposite.

As he stood and looked, the man next to him chuckled, then announced, 'It must have been a bloody nightmare to have been stuck in that when it went over.'

He did not respond. He considered it best to remain anonymous. He had wondered about all his personal belongings still in cupboards on the boat, but then another comment put his mind at rest.

'You'd have to be desperate to wade in that mud to get to it.'

He walked up and down the towpath, inspecting the length of the boat, and decided all was OK. It was just at a strange angle… There was nothing he could do about it apart from wait for the professionals to sort it.

Mistakenly he thought it would be simple: seal the hole in the canal bottom, let the water in and watch his boat float on top of the water. Bingo: back to normal.

After several phone calls to several departments he managed to make an appointment to see the local engineer, who informed him of the complexities of refloating sunken craft.

Albert met the jobsworth from the waterways department, and they stood on the bank assessing the situation. With the aid of a sketch the jobsworth advised him that if the canal *was* refilled with water, his boat would simply fill with water also, and remain on the bottom, thus making it a hazard to other boat owners.

'We could put signs with arrows on them advising boat owners to avoid the sunken wreck,' the jobsworth said, 'because that's what it would be after a fortnight in canal water. So it would be better if it were removed prior to the water being let back in.'

As the happy man left he added another point for consideration.

'Heavy lifting gear will be needed. I hope thy bloody insurance is up to date.'

'What insurance?' Albert thought.

***

He stared at number two on his list. It had bothered him more than the upturning of his boat. It was the simple but important matter of the humiliation after the sinking: the picture – his picture – on the front page in the local press. This matter required a kind of 'an eye for an eye and a tooth for a tooth' kind of getting even. The ribbing from fellow drinkers in his local had settled down, but deep inside it rankled. He still felt that people were talking and laughing behind his back, and making whispered remarks: 'That's that man who went under the mud and got his picture in the paper.'

In large capital letters, he wrote,

SORT OUT THAT BASTARD REPORTER

then highlighted it with a marker pen.

Digger and Spade: progress?

The investigation was moving on, and Digger and Spade decided to move on to the crime of brutal murder inflicted on the boy. The pub was not open when they arrived, and so they hammered on the door. They heard the barman shout, 'OK … OK,' as he unfastened the many locks.

'Yes,' he barked as he opened the door a fraction. 'We are not open yet. Come back in an hour. Will your thirst last that long?' he added mockingly.

The two detectives looked at one another as they reached inside their coats for their warrant cards.

'Why didn't you say? Think I'm a bleeding mind reader?'

'Less of the lip. Is it gonna be here or the station?'

'Is it what?'

'It is the interview about a murder that happened on your doorstep, and the possibility that you may be able to help us solve who did it.'

Once inside, the barman, who was obviously in a foul mood, returned to his side of the bar and carried on cleaning. They followed him into the pub and started quizzing him about the night of the murder, but because he was preparing to open up, he ignored them.

'Put the soddin' glass down. This is serious business,' barked DI Digger.

'Crikey. Keep your hair on. I have to open the door to a thirsty mob in five minutes. Look, I've told all I know to the other coppers who came round the other day. Do you not keep records?'

'No, so tell us again.'

'Right. This big, awful git – who looked like a builder, or something – just got himself pissed, gave me some verbal then staggered out at the end of the night.'

'Go on.'

'He just went. Called me some horrible name as he went past. I locked up after he walked through the door.'

'So you didn't hear anything, didn't catch his name?'

'Not a thing.'

'For Christ's sake, man. A murder is committed right outside your door, and you didn't hear anything?'

'Look: he gets himself pissed, he answers a couple of calls, he falls asleep… Then when I wake him up he gives me grief. That's it.'

'OK. If you remember anything, give us a call,' said Digger, and handed him a card.

As they stepped out onto the pavement they spotted Simon and Reginald walking towards the pub.

'Good Jesus, there are some weirdos round here,' muttered Spade.

'What did I tell you? Throttle is full of them.'

'Aye, but look where they're going. The pub's not open yet.'

They turned to see Reginald and Simon sweep into the now unlocked front door of the pub.

'We're not open yet… Be about ten minutes,' shouted the barman, who was now working at the rear of the pub, when he heard them enter. Moments later, among the barrels and the odour of stale beer, the barman turned to see Reginald and Simon staring at him.

'What the frig do you want?'

'You,' was the short reply.

There was no escape. They had him cornered by the empties. Reginald pushed him to the floor, then pointed to Simon.

'OK, over to you.'

'If I let this barrel drop on you…' Simon threatened.

'You'll need more than a frigging dentist,' added Reginald. 'Wouldn't you rather talk to us? Then he can put the barrel down.'

'What do you want?'

'Rumour has it that you entertained a punter the other night who is suspected of being involved with the flooding and the murder. We need a name.'

'Richard, he was called. That's all. Heard him say that the job had gone according to plan. No witnesses.'

It was then that Simon slipped on a slimy, beer-stained flagstone, and dropped the barrel on the barman's foot.

'I don't know any more. Oh, God, I'm going to faint!' he screamed.

They helped him inside, sat him down in a chair and casually walked through the front door.

'Lot of effort just to get a name,' said Simon.

***

Back in the building site hut, which was now renamed the S & R Detective Agency Communications Room, they reviewed the incident in the pub.

'You could have killed him.'

'I were getting tired. You should learn to talk faster.'

Reginald and Simon stared at the four panes on the door that had been erected in the middle of their office.

'So,' Simon announced while removing the top from his felt pen, 'we have a big bloke wearing loads of gold – probably a double murderer – with muddy boots, and his name is Richard or Big Dick.'

'And he drives a four-by-four and can drive a digger,' added Reginald.

On the first pane of glass Simon sketched the shape of a man sitting on a tractor wearing a big watch.

'Yes. Very good. And we also have a witness, who very kindly gave us Richard or Big Dick's number. But now he can't sleep at night, cos you threatened to kill him.'

'For clarification, he can't sleep because he is involved in a murder and has a friend who is a murderer – and, yes, we have spoken to him and threatened to murder him.'

'OK. Progress,' added Simon, as he drew a face on the glass with wild eyes and scary hair.

'This is not a frigging game, you know. Lots of money – our money – is at stake here… And another thing … we have another witness, who says he heard him saying he had done the job with no witnesses, but who now has a crushed foot.' Reginald, now tiring of the activity, turned to the kettle.

'Brew?'

'Always. But it's not my fault. You went on a bit.'

'OK, OK. We have a big bloke – a murderer, probably a double murderer… Well, somebody needs to ring him.'

'Scary. Stuff that … maybe we should report in first.'

'Good idea. Get Lagg's number.'

Joe Lagg held the phone to his ear, but could not believe what he heard. 'Are you out of your mind? I do not ring mud-covered psychopaths. You – the heavy mob – do that. I do the technical. Remember?'

'So what do we ask him? Are you a double murderer? Why did you try to drown a whole village?'

'Close. Just ask him why he went to all that trouble to send the canal down our drains.'

'Shall I use your name?'

'Bog off. Don't use any name to a psychopath.'

After a well-earned brew the two newly appointed detectives sat at the desk staring at the phone.

'Go on then,' urged Simon.

Not knowing who would answer, Reginald dialled the number.

'Hello, there. Is that Richard?' said Reginald, trying to sound official.

'Who's this?' said the gruff voice.

'Never mind who it is. We just need a few answers. Don't hang up.'

'I'll bleeding hang you if I get hold of you.'

Reginald took a sharp intake of breath as his mind raced.

'We know all about you: your description, the car you drive, the two lads you killed, what you did up at Fossit's farm … The point is, we don't know why.'

Richard with the gruff voice paused. Reginald could hear him breathing heavily.

'It were just a job. Went a bit wrong, that's all. Accident, like.'

'Sometimes jobs do go wrong,' replied Reginald, trying to soften him. 'So you were working for someone else?'

'Aye.'

'Who?' Reginald asked.

The phone clicked off.

'Bugger. Just as I thought he was going to open up.'

'So, an accident-prone psychopath … the worst kind,' said Simon.

'You should know,' replied Reginald.

Three a.m. A man too long without sleep

The man who lived next door to the Costain family had difficulty sleeping. A late-evening fillet steak meal with all the trimmings accompanied by a bottle of red wine, a cheese board, and coffee to finish had taken its toll on his digestive system.

'I'm going to make a brew,' he whispered to his comatose wife while holding his stomach. She snored on. As he was filling the kettle and staring through the kitchen window into the darkness he thought he could hear a scraping noise, but put it down to nocturnal goings-on.

'You get a lot of it round here: badgers, foxes, cats, stray dogs … like a bloody menagerie,' he thought as he waited for the kettle to boil. However, as he poured out the water and the noise from the kettle subsided, he definitely did hear something. And it was close.

He carefully parted the curtain, and then dropped the scalding cup of tea onto his bare feet. The resultant scream alerted his wife who, on arrival, suggested he should firstly immerse his foot in a bowl of cold water then, secondly, seek the help of a psychiatrist.

'Keep your foot under. The pain will go away eventually,' his wife advised him, with little sympathy. 'Then you can tell me again about the hooded man in white.'

'I tell you, it were the Grim Reaper. He had a spade in his hand.'

'The Grim Reaper carries a scythe, and he wears black,' she laughed.

'Not round here he doesn't.'

It took a while for the pain to subside sufficiently for him to be able to return to bed.

***

Meanwhile, John Costain sat in the garage until his neighbour's lights went out. Then he crept gingerly round the front of his house and carried on scraping and bagging the soil. Normally an activity like this would be achieved quickly, but doing it so as not to arouse anyone meant it dragged on till the birds started to sing. He put the equipment required for the task back in the black bags and shoved it under a bench in the garage.

'She will never notice this' he thought. Every movement seemed to make a noise as he crept upstairs then back into the marital bed. He tried his best not to disturb the sheets as he slid in alongside his wife. Before he nodded off, he smiled, because he thought she was unaware.

He should have known better.

The case goes cold

At nine thirty a.m. Digger and Spade were sitting in their cramped office, files of unsolved crimes piled on either side of their desks. On Digger's desk the latest file perched on top had this title:

Double murder at Throttle

'Had the boss on this morning,' Digger sighed. 'He says if we don't solve something soon we're going to be transferred to Inverness, out of the way.'

'We had a cat called Inverness once,' added Spade.

Digger looked up.

'It was a cold and miserable bastard,' Spade laughed.

They tipped out the contents of the file and rummaged through the scant information.

'For God's sake,' said Digger exasperatedly, 'there's got to be something. First millions and millions of gallons of water get piped into the sewage system, then they find a body, then within hours another body ... and nobody knows anything. Let's start again.'

Digger took out a coin from his pocket.

'Heads the pub; tails the farm.'

An hour or so later they knocked on the pub door. The barman peered round the edge of the door. Lines of strain were visible on his forehead.

'What?' he croaked.

'We'd like to ask you some more questions.'

'More? What for?'

They both peered down at the gleaming white plaster on the barman's ankle.

'What happened to you?'

'Two blokes asked me the same questions you did. Then, when I said I didn't know any more, they did this.'

Digger and Spade both beamed.

'Timing… It's all about timing. If we hadn't decided to start again, we wouldn't know about this,' Digger said, smiling and pointing towards the plastered ankle.

'It's not funny. I were lucky to get away with this. He could have killed me.'

'Ah! Movement,' said Digger. 'Another interested party. Now things are happening. So what did you tell them?'

'Only what I told you.'

'You told us nothing. Do you want the other foot doing?'

The barman held the plaster as if to soothe the pulsating ankle.

'I need to sit down. This is frigging killing me.'

He shuffled to a table, sat down and rested his ankle on another chair.

'They were nutters. It's all going wrong in Throttle. It used to be a quiet town, with nothing happening. Now it's full of nutters and psychopaths, and I'm in the middle of it.'

He took out a bottle of pills and shakily dispensed himself two painkillers.

'We are full of sympathy, we really are, and your ankle will get better,' said Digger unconvincingly. 'But we need to solve this case in a hurry. So – again – what mysteriously came to mind when this man held a barrel over you? What did you tell him that you couldn't tell us? Oh, and by the way, withholding evidence is a criminal offence: a metaphorical barrel, if you like.'

The barman gripped his leg and winced.

'It was only what I overheard him say on the phone. He said his name was Richard and that the job was done, and there were no witnesses.'

'So why did you not tell us this before?'

'Because he's probably a double murderer, and I don't want to be number three. It's frigging obvious.'

They nodded and stood up.

'We will leave you to your convalescence, but if you think of anything else…' said Digger.

'Don't forget: thud, click … the other ankle,' added Spade as he demonstrated the falling of a barrel.

***

In the car they perused the limited notes.

'Threats and violence. That's much better,' said Digger, flicking over his notepad as they drove away.

'Now let's go and see that farmer again. If the same two nutters have visited him as well, then they might have loosened his tongue a bit too.'

Moments later they were driving down the rough track leading to the farm when, as they went past a gate hole, they heard a gunshot. They instinctively ducked down, braked hard and then heard the sound of the contents of a twelve-bore cartridge whizz overhead.

They waited a while until they thought the coast was clear.

'Hell of a place, this. Inverness is looking attractive,' muttered Spade.

They raised their heads and peered through the

windscreen. They reeled back in their seats as they saw the farmer approach, carrying a shotgun.

'Sorry, sorry. I was shooting at a fox,' he shouted, still pointing the smoking gun.

'"Sorry, sorry." Are you frigging mad? Point it the other way. You pepper the sodding car, then say you are sorry?'

'Couldn't see the car. I was aiming at the fox.'

The farmer pointed the gun to the floor, then flicked out the spent cartridge. As he looked up they saw the grief in his watery eyes.

'I've not slept. They said they would kill me if I spoke to anyone.'

'Explain.'

'The big bastard said he would kill me if I spoke to anyone, then these other odd-looking bastards said they would kill me if I didn't talk.'

'So... Get many foxes round here, do you?'

'No ... not many.'

Digger beamed again.

'Things are really looking up. Now tell me again. Who are these people?' he said, taking hold of the gun from the farmer's trembling hand.

One for the road

On a flight to Leeds Bradford Airport, a man with a sunburnt face was drinking to steady his nerves. His gold bracelet shook and rattled noisily as he tried to get a glass of spirit to his lips. The man sitting next to him couldn't help but stare.

'You OK?' he enquired.

The man with the sunburnt face turned, opened his mouth, then thought before speaking. The man sitting next to him watched as he searched for the right words.

'Good point. Not sure. I was OK up to about a fortnight ago, then things went – how shall I say – a bit pear-shaped.'

He looked through the window at the clouds for inspiration before he said anything else. He had been considering recent events and how he could solve the issue – or, alternatively, disown the man who had gone beyond his remit. The problem was that he had had no one to run it by, until now.

'Can I run a hypothetical situation by you?' he asked.

The stranger nodded and agreed.

'Hypothetical, you say?'

'Oh, yes. Anyway, this chap – a friend of mine – was on holiday, and while he was away he got this other bloke to sort out a problem.'

'What sort of problem?' asked the stranger.

'Oh, nothing much. Just a bit of debt collecting,' he reassured the stranger. 'So, anyway, this bloke doing the debt collecting decided on a method that was – how shall I say? – a bit on the heavy side.'

'What do you mean by "heavy"?' asked the stranger.

'Not heavy in the sense of weight. More heavy in the sense of grave.'

'Grave … I see.'

'You see, what this chap – my friend – had not counted on was the fact – and he only found out later – that this bloke was not really a full shilling.'

The stranger put his finger to the side of his head and nodded.

'I see. A slate loose.'

'Precisely. Anyway, he acted beyond his remit.'

'Do nutcases have remits?' he smirked.

'Well, anyway, all this chap – the friend of mine – asked him to do was to collect a debt, but in the process he went a bit far.'

'I see. Bit too heavy … a bit grave,' added the stranger, getting into the story.

'Well, aye.'

The man with the red face stared through the window again.

'Anyway, it's only a suspicion, but my friend thinks that the man with the loose slate is the cause of two unfortunate deaths.'

The stranger furrowed his brow, pursed his lips and inhaled.

'For being responsible for two unfortunate deaths do we read being responsible for murder?'

'That's what this chap – my friend – thought, but he didn't want this to happen. He just asked for a debt to be recovered.'

'Did this chap – friend of yours – pay a fee to the nutcase with the remit?'

'I'm afraid so.'

'Then this chap – er, your friend – is implicated in the grave, er, two unfortunate deaths stroke murders.'

The stranger noticed the concern written across the man's red face.

'So what is this chap going to do?'

'He is going to have a meeting with him to find out what went on.'

The stranger took a further sharp intake of breath.

'Jesus … so let me get this straight. This chap – your friend – is going to have a meeting with a murdering nutcase, who apparently couldn't give a shit about a remit, in order to find out if he is implicated in what the said nutcase has done.'

The red-faced man adopted a sickly grin and nodded.

'Does this chap not consider that he might become number three in order to preserve the said murdering nutcase's freedom?'

'He said it had gone through his mind.'

'Did he? Well, best of frigging British,' added the stranger as he pulled the free newspaper towards him.

The grieving is superseded by a desire for justice (revenge)

The two fathers of the murdered sons had agreed to meet at the local. They sat stony-faced, neither wanting to make the first move. With alcohol being the other common denominator in the meeting it seemed only correct that they should savour their beer in silence before a discussion could begin.

'The coppers have been round. They know nowt,' said one.

'Aye. They've been round to our house. The wife screamed blue murder at them. Said if they couldn't come up with summat she would do a sit-in at the station.'

Another pint provided the courage they needed to start their own investigations.

'We can't just sit around waiting. The culprit will be long gone. As I see it, that idiot of a farmer must know something. We should start there.'

'Aye. He's as much to blame, letting the bastard dig the trench. Come on, let's go and sort him out.'

***

In the meantime, Farmer Fossit had been to the supermarket and stocked up with provisions for a siege: simple fare, which consisted of baked beans, cans of beer, bread, milk and tea bags. He also called at the gunsmith to stock up on more cartridges.

'Are you sure?' queried the man in the gunsmith's.

'Aye. All of a sudden I'm overrun with vermin.'

On the outside of the farmhouse, as part of the security measures, he had nailed wooden pallets over the ground-floor windows and plywood sheeting across the back door to prevent a surprise ambush. He had positioned his armchair next to the only window that would open in the event of an attack.

Then he waited, newly cleaned double-barrelled shotgun at the ready. Being the only sentry on the 'fortress' meant staying awake at all times, but the comfort of the armchair made it difficult to stay alert. He had only been doing it for twenty-four hours but already he had begun to understand the meaning of sleep deprivation. As his eyelids began to close a tear slid down his face. Then, as he realised he was slipping into a depressed mood, he sat bolt upright and shouted, 'Come on, you bastards. I'm ready for you.' He sniffed and cocked the hammers of the twelve-bore.

***

It was fortunate timing for the two fathers to approach down the rough track to the farmhouse. Luckily for them he could see their heads bobbing up and down as they approached from the other side of a dry-stone wall, well before they got close enough for an accurate shot.

All he could see through tearful eyes was two characters approaching the house. To him they were the enemy. He opened the window before taking aim. He squinted, then let loose with an overhead warning blast that knocked him to the back of the armchair. They immediately dropped to the floor and sat with their backs to the wall.

'This is not going as planned. And, as the saying goes, we should live to fight another day.'

They stooped lower than the height of the wall and ran as fast as the position would allow. The farmer grinned, and opened another can of beer. Breathless and sweating, they paused in a gate opening.

'The man's a lunatic.'

'There's got to be an easier way of doing this – at least one that doesn't get you shot to bits. Better give it some thought over a pint, eh?'

'Well, we tried. At least I can tell my wife we tried.'

A friendly voice

Albert had given the subject of getting even with the reporters a lot of thought, and decided that he could combine that with helping an old friend in the process. Unfortunately for him the farmer was in a deep sleep. Graham Fossit was beginning to lose it. After being startled by the ringing phone he pointed the gun at it and shouted, 'Go away. I'm not in.'

Albert had to ring twice before he got an answer.

'Hello there, Graham. How you doing?' said Albert, shouting down the phone.

Fossit grabbed his gun and pointed it at the phone while holding the receiver in his other hand.

'Who are you?' he bawled.

'It's Albert, Albert Bradley. You remember ... we used to go to school together.'

'Bloody hell, that's fifty years ago. What do you want?'

'Hey, steady on a bit. I'm here to help.'

Graham Fossit got angrier.

'Nobody rings or comes round here unless they want summat. Now what do you want?' he ranted.

'Now look, I'm just ringing to see if I can help out, that's all... You know ... old friends, like. Can I come round? Only it's a dear do on the phone.'

'I expect so.'

'Now you're talking. Put the kettle on.'

An hour or so later Albert knocked on the front door, and then stared through the letterbox. He saw Graham Fossit standing behind the door aiming the gun at him.

'Eh up. It's only me. Put the bleeding gun down.'

'Sorry. Not sure who calls these days.'

While he undid the many bolts and locks Albert looked around at the fortifications. The hour or so it took for Albert to arrive had given Graham a chance to tidy up a bit. As he opened the door a burnt cabbage odour hit his nostrils.

'Good God. What's that smell?' Albert asked, holding his nose.

'Oh, that. Been living on baked beans for a few days. Burnt a few pans. Kept getting distracted … not the best idea I've ever had.'

He stroked the stubble on his face, then sniffed himself under the arms. 'Not been able to have a bath or owt in case they break in. I tried having a shower while holding the gun, but with the soap an' all I kept losing my grip. I thought, "If this goes off in here, I'm buggered!"'

Albert left open the door, entered and opened the only window that worked.

'Let's get some air through.'

Once the air had freshened they sat in front of the fire with a mug of tea.

'There are some horrible rumours going round.'

'Oh?'

'You've been firing at folk. The word is that you're losing your marbles.'

'Well, I've had two lots of thugs threatening to kill me, and other nosy parkers. I've had the police round here twice. They don't seem to believe what I'm saying – and all the suspicions about that dead lad are on my doorstep, so to speak – and the chances are that they'll all be round here again.'

He took a mouthful of tea then continued. 'So do you understand why I'm barricaded in my own house and holding a gun? I haven't slept for ages.'

As he spoke his bottom lip began to tremble and his eyes filled up.

'I tell you, someone's going to get both barrels before very long.'

Albert watched as Graham's fingers twitched over the gun's mechanism.

'Hey, cut that out,' shouted Albert, although there was an element of support in his voice. Then he pointed out a home truth about the weapon.

'Good God, man. Once you've stuffed a person with that thing they stay stuffed. Harm somebody with that and they will lock you up and throw away the key,' he added with a hint of humour.

Graham wiped his eyes with his hanky and blew his nose.

'It's all getting out of control. I've done nowt wrong. I'm just a bystander in all this … being bleeding interrogated and threatened by thugs and nutters.'

Albert gave him a few minutes to calm down then reassured him. 'Don't worry. We'll sort it out. You're just a victim of strange circumstances. First things first. You go and have a bath and a lie down, and I'll stand guard.'

Albert took the gun, broke it at the hinge, flicked out the cartridges and stood it in a corner.

'I don't know why you're doing it, but I do appreciate it. I don't think I could go on much longer.'

Albert looked through into the kitchen at a pile of burnt pans in the sink and said, 'Tea and toast from now on. No more baked beans for you.'

It was the ice-breaker they both needed, and although they did not howl with laughter they afforded a grin to one another.

***

Graham trudged off upstairs, and Albert made himself comfortable in the armchair. He peered through the window and through the gap in the wooden pallet. He had to squint and adjusted his position in order to see down the track.

'He's lucky to see anything, never mind intruders,' he observed to himself.

It wasn't long before he also succumbed to the soporific effect of the lookout position. The squeaking floorboards from the room above, though, alerted him that Graham was on the move after a bath and a short nap. Albert sat bolt upright and leant towards the window to give the impression he had not lapsed in his duty.

'You can hardly see anything here,' he said as Graham entered the room.

'If you get your eye in the right place you can see right down the track… See 'em coming … see 'em before they see you,' he said.

'Can't keep this up, though. It's mindless. What is needed is an intruder alarm, a trap of some kind … so what's in the big tank?' he asked, pointing towards a large round metal tank in the farmyard.

'Slurry.'

Albert looked puzzled.

'It's shit. It's from when I had cattle about four or five years ago. It's still full.'

'It's enormous. Why on earth would you keep that

much?'

'The idea is that at the back end of the year you spray it on the field as a fertiliser. But in reality you did it just to get rid of it.'

'Should be nicely matured by now,' Albert grinned.

'I just couldn't be bothered to do anything with it. There's lots on this farm that I can't be bothered about.' As he spoke, he yawned loudly. 'Sorry. I'm going to have to go and get some more shut-eye. I feel absolutely knackered.'

'Not a problem. I'll keep watch.'

He listened as Graham set foot up the creaky staircase, then when he thought he had finally gone to bed he had a nosy round the outbuildings. When he was in his teens he had helped on various farms, so the sights and smells were no stranger to him. It was hard work. Everything was done by hand, and the farmers had a reputation of being tight-fisted. It took a while, but once the novelty of attending to other people's animals wore off – and it became obvious there would be no money in it – he stopped going.

The one thing he was curious about was the fact that everywhere you went it was full of manure.

It came from all the stock, including chickens and geese. It was a full-time job dealing with it. It was swept out of the pens, piled up into heaps, put into a tank and then spread on the field so you could walk in it. Then it came back to the farm on your shoes and the whole cycle started again. You got full of it. It got on your clothes, everywhere.

'My mother used to play hell,' he said to himself. 'Been on that smelly farm again? Well, leave your clothes out in the back,' he could recall her shouting.

'Nothing has changed,' he said as he negotiated the dark puddles. He was also amazed by the farmers' careless attitude to machinery and equipment. 'If a piece of tackle breaks down or runs out of fuel, they just leave it where it stands: tractors, ploughs, all just left in the field in all weathers. You see them in fields rotting away, then they plead bleeding poverty.'

***

He pulled open the tall door of another barn and peeked inside. To his delight he spotted something in the corner that brightened his day.

At first it looked abandoned. Covered in the obligatory straw and red rust was a tractor, but not any old tractor. He wandered into the darkened barn and felt his way round to the front of the machine. As he wiped off the dust from the badge on the radiator cowl he could clearly see the word 'Ferguson'. He opened both the large doors of the barn to shed more light on his find. The sun streaming through the open door picked out the dust in the atmosphere. He waved his hand across his face to aid his breathing and as the dust settled it became apparent to a tractor buff what it was.

'Bleedin' hell ... a grey Fergy,' he beamed as he sat in the cold perforated metal seat and cranked the steering wheel back and forth. His recollections of driving one as a teenager were mixed.

'These tractors did not have any suspension and were responsible for giving farmers back problems, but they were fun to drive.'

He continued with his commentary as if speaking to an audience.

'Complete with hydraulic bucket ... very collectable,

so long as it works,' he muttered with authority.

Moments later he was checking the engine for missing components.

'Farmers were useless mechanics. They mended everything with pliers or a hammer,' he added as he tugged at the plug leads. Once he considered the tractor serviceable, his mind raced as he ticked the boxes of a method of retribution against the *Throttle Flyer*.

'Revenge is a dish best served sloppy and cold,' he mused.

***

Later, after Graham had surfaced, they sat and watched the flames of the fire.

'You don't look like a tractor nut,' mumbled Graham as he slurped his tea.

'What does one look like?'

'Probably grey hair, a flat cap and a boiler suit that's seen better days.'

'I'm nearly there. And don't forget a spanner. You always had to have a spanner at the ready. They used to break down for fun. You should be grateful that I've unearthed it. It's a Ferguson TE20… not in bad nick … be collectable when we're done.'

Graham gave him a nod of approval about his knowledge.

'Anyway, what do you reckon? It looks all there. The tyres are a bit soft, but that's easily sorted. We could solve both our problems in one easy go: get those bastards off your back, and settle an old score for me.'

Graham smiled.

'Sounds good to me. I'm ready for a change of diet.'

'Thank God for that,' said Albert.

Duty calls

Reginald and Simon assumed their position as gatekeepers to the building site. In response to the damage caused by the flood and the potential for further vandalism by unknown parties they thought it wise to vet the incoming builders to the site. They had organised an additional troop of workers to attend to the water damage created by the flood.

Industrial-type dehumidifiers were installed in each house and left running until the rooms were dry, and to keep track of this latest addition to the workload they had positioned on the wall a spreadsheet indicating the house number, the damage and the likely date the work would be completed. This methodical arrangement had been on the instructions of Joe Lagg, who also had an identical spreadsheet on his wall. The other dictate had been that it must be updated daily to his secretary.

The side job of being detectives had tapered off because of the lack of leads. The progress board, now gathering dust, still had only two names on it: those of Richard and of the farmer.

'Nowt else we can do at the moment. Time to have a tidy up, what with all these distractions … just look at this mountain of mail.'

They decided on a brew first. Then, when the motivation kicked in, they got organised. Reginald reached for the cardboard box marked 'In tray' in thick felt pen.

'You open the envelopes and pass them to me. If it's rubbish - and, more than likely it will be - I'll put it straight in the bin.'

'And if it's not?' asked Simon.

'Then we will soddin' well have to read it. That's what mail is about.'

'But how do we know if it's rubbish or not till we have read it?'

'You can tell. If it's junk mail it will be adverts - pictures and such.'

'OK. Easy,' added Simon.

They worked their way through the mail until they arrived at two large brown envelopes. Simon held them up.

'I think these have gone to the wrong address,' he announced.

'Why?'

'Because it just says, *For the attention of the idiots in charge.*'

'How long have these been here?'

'Ages. They were right at the bottom of the pile.'

'Didn't you think to open them?'

'Too busy: work, work, busy, busy, bang, bang,' grinned Simon. 'Besides, I don't recognise the address. Do you?'

Reginald snatched them from him, ripped open the ends and emptied the contents onto the desk.

'Jesus,' they gawped.

The letters consisted of two sheets, each with a message using letters cut out of newspapers. The first read: *Pay the £50,000 you owe within ten days or get your wellies on.*

The next one read: *Next is the fire. Pay up, or get your extinguishers ready.*

Reginald stared at them a while.

'Oh dear, oh dear, oh dear. This is getting serious. Obviously the first one is now out of date.'

'It was a lot of trouble to go to … to cut out all them letters and stick them down. Why not just write it? Must have taken ages … some kind of a nut.'

'Excuse me? We have a murdering arsonist in our midst, and you are worrying about the method of the manufacture of the threatening letter?'

'Just wondering, that's all. Trying to get inside the mind of the criminal brain. Do you think there is a biblical element to it? Flood and fire, if you get my drift.'

Reginald pointed to the phone. 'Get Lagg.'

Simon got Lagg.

'You'd better come round, Mr Lagg. I think we have stumbled across something.'

They displayed the letters to Joe Lagg, who immediately panicked and started to wave his arms around.

'Who is it? Who do we owe money to, this kind of money? Fifty grand, for God's sake,' he barked.

They stared at the window, then the ceiling, then the floor.

'Come on … electricians, plumbers, joiners, brickies? Who have we not paid? Anyway, whoever it is thinks he deserves a bonus and is quite prepared to put us out of business.'

'Murder … don't forget the murder,' added Simon, with effect.

Joe turned and looked at Simon with contempt.

'We are dealing with an irrational, psychopathic killer,

and his threatening letters are buried under your mail.'

They looked at Simon.

'You're first in every morning. It's dead easy: put the kettle on, pick up the mail, flick through it to see if there's anything worth looking at – like a death threat – but no. You pick it up and dump it, to be read later.'

'Timescale,' said Reginald as he tried to take the heat away from Simon.

They looked at him.

'Timescale. We had the demand: it expired. We had the threat of the flood: it went ahead. Now we have the threat of fire. Where are we in the timescale of the ten days?'

'We don't know where we are with the timescale, and we don't know who to send the money to. Brilliant. Well, Holmes and Watson, you'd better get your skates and thinking caps on or there'll be nothing but a pile of ashes to look after.'

'Who's who?' asked Simon.

The late-night landscaping had not gone unnoticed

'My Jack was really spooked the other night,' said Mrs Costain's neighbour in a moment of idle gossip.

'He's not been the same since. He said he saw the Grim Reaper ... the thing was ... he said he was all in white, and instead of a scythe he had a shovel. He was so shocked he burnt his foot.' She folded her arms and rocked them side to side as she waited for a response.

'On purpose? He burnt his foot on purpose?'

'No. He jumped while holding the kettle.'

'Do you think Grim Reapers change their appearance for different countries? You know, black for abroad and white for here?'

Mystified, Mrs Costain just stood and stared and did her best not to burst into laughter.

'He's taken to the drink. He's shaking all the time. Says his time must be up.'

Mrs Costain was looking out of the kitchen window later when she spotted a freshly dug patch of garden minus the tulips she had fed and watered. She ventured out and stood at what had once been a small patch of garden with a neat border around it. She pursed her lips, raised her eyebrows and followed the trail of soil. She opened the door that led into the back of the garage. Tucked away under the bench she spotted two new shiny black bin bags. She untied the knot and opened the bag.

'What are you up to?' John shouted as she rummaged in a sack.

She turned, held up the white boiler suit and stared at him.

'What are *you* up to, more like?'

Later, up on the cut

John wandered up the canal bank towards Robert's boat. This time it was early evening, and although it was not fully daylight it did allow a good look round. Boats were moored nose to tail as far as you could see – all seemingly occupied, according to the smoke oozing from the chimneys. But the windows appeared blacked out to anyone passing by. He stopped and stared at one boat. It was tilting over so much it looked as if it was sinking. Then a curtain twitched and a face appeared.

'Sorry,' he apologised. 'I'm just looking for a friend's boat.'

He walked on until he found Robert's boat.

'Bleeding hell,' he thought.

Every part of the roof was used for storage: wood piled high, dead plants in pots, old bikes, tarpaulins and empty gas cylinders. Then he turned. Each boat had an adjacent plot of land, more storage for kindling, more old bikes and raised beds containing plants that seemed to be past their best.

'What do you think?' asked Robert as he poked his head out of the hatch.

'Not sure. I'm trying to work it out,' he said as he looked around at what was to him just disorganised garbage.

'Does it all work, this self-sufficiency lark?'

Robert sighed.

'Depends on your needs. Most of the people round here all have different creative skills, so if you are in need of something it can always be obtained… To a certain extent it's more about cooperation: a bit of bartering or trade, if you like. You coming in?'

As he climbed on board he wondered about the boats in darkness with their curtains drawn. They looked abandoned but had smoke oozing out of the chimneys, which suggested that someone lived on them.

'I didn't know this existed. How many people live here?'

'Hard to say. People come and go. The boats stay, but people come and go.'

'Right … transient, gypsy-like?'

'Afraid it's not as romantic as that. I don't pry, but most are escaping from something or someone.'

John looked puzzled.

'The law?'

'Look … it is a community, but we are a bit more relaxed than most … relationships, tax, debt … and the use of substances that make life more bearable.'

'Oh… I see.' There was a pause.

It had just dawned on John that Robert had appeared from his boat without him knocking on the roof.

'Anyway, how did you know I was here?' he added, to break the silence.

'Jungle drums. You were spotted as soon as you arrived on the bank. You must have appeared furtive, and people get twitchy when they spot someone being nosy.'

'Yeah. Furtive, that's me. How long is the boat?' he enquired as they went through the narrow passageway.

'Seventy feet,' Robert replied casually.

'Good Jesus. So we are only in the kitchen.'

'Galley,' Robert corrected him. 'Yeah. There's a lounge, a bathroom, a bedroom and a workshop.'

Although he had been before, he felt more relaxed and able to look around this time.

'Very smart, this,' he complimented Robert as he ran his finger over the highly polished brass porthole. 'It's a contrast to the outside,' he added, more as a question than an observation.

'Ah … we like to give the impression of a community that is perhaps living a lower quality of life than it actually is.'

'Why?' he asked bluntly.

'Community tax, road tax, income tax, value added tax, inheritance tax and not forgetting capital gains tax.'

'I see.' As they walked through into the lounge, the quality of the furniture impressed him. 'Wide-screen TV, comfy seats, and central heating… Bloody hell. It's better than our house.'

'Fancy a beer?'

They reminisced for quite a while, then Robert asked the question they both had been skirting round.

'What are we going to do about your house?'

'Don't know. I've not got much experience in these matters.'

'So, cards on the table. The house: you can't live in it, you can't sell it and you dare not broadcast it.'

'Pretty much,' he replied with resignation.

'There was obviously no mention of the asbestos when you bought it, then?'

'No mention at all. In fact everyone involved was very aware of it being a brownfield site and, as such, there were rules and regs to be followed.'

'Then it's quite likely that the people at the council planning kept it quiet. So did the solicitors, the estate agents, the tenants in the units – and, finally – the landowner.'

'Bastards!' John said, raising his voice.

'They will all have received bungs,' added Robert.

'Bungs?'

'Brown envelopes, kickbacks – call it what you want. It happens all the time. They all piss in the same pot and go to the same club.'

'Really? What can we do?'

'We can get you your money back.'

'That would be great, but how? You can't sue them, can you?'

'No, but there are other ways … That is, if you'll let us. Of course, we'll need your permission.'

'Us?'

'Yeah. It's a group of us who take on challenges like this. We try to support causes where we think people have been stuffed by so-called entrepreneurs. There's a lot of it about, especially when it comes to landowners … it's been going on for hundreds of years.'

John could hear Robert getting onto his soapbox, and although he was interested he sensed time was getting on.

'I see… Well, yes… If you can help us out, get us our money and our life back … go ahead. What will it cost?'

'Just think of it as one mate doing a favour for another. Fancy another?' he added, holding up a beer can. John accepted the hospitality but, as he drank, he was suspicious about what he was sanctioning.

'Are you OK?' asked Robert as he sensed caution in John's voice.

'Yeah. It's just that this is new territory for me.'

'Then it's just as well that you came here first.'

Partially reassured, John offered a watery smile and rushed his drink.

***

Soon after, as he left the boat and walked down the embankment, a casually dressed lady held her breath while hiding behind a dilapidated polytunnel. In an instant her concerns regarding her husband's activities were swapped for memories of herself as a teenager.

'It can't be him,' she thought.

As she crept out of hiding she was taken aback by the owner's name on the side of the boat.

'Surely not *that* Robert?' she thought.

She reminisced about her college days. Days of carefree and reckless activity ... days when she did not have to do chores and cleaning all day.

'Hello? I could do without this. The last thing I need is someone from the past causing a distraction. I'm a lady with responsibilities: a home, everyday jobs ... a child, for goodness' sake,' she shouted, louder than she wanted to. 'Well, not on your life,' she added with disapproval.

As she held on to the steel post that supported the polytunnel she felt the chill of the early evening. It was difficult to erase the memory of her college days from her mind.

In an effort to distract her mind she started looking around inside the tunnel.

'Nothing to speak of here,' she said to herself. 'Just a load of dead plants.'

As she inspected the remnants of the efforts of self-sufficiency she failed to notice the rocking of the boat that indicated those on board were active. As Robert emerged she heard the click of the padlock on his cabin door. She spun around, looked back and could just see the rear of his dreadlocked head as he walked swiftly down the embankment.

'It is him, I think!' she exhaled loudly. 'It is him. Same name, though it is ages ago. His hair has changed. Wonder what he's up to. Is he married? If he was, then her name would be on the boat as well.'

She ran the evidence through her mind ... all the possibilities of the happenings since then, ten years ago.

Recently, since moving into the new house, she had gained an interest in gardening. So she was puzzled. As she looked around, all the plants seemed lifeless.

'It's easy. Just put them in, keep them well watered and fed, and they grow like crazy. So what's going on here?'

She stooped to inspect the limp foliage of a half-dead plant with several spiky leaves.

'So that's how they spend the long winter evenings,' she smiled.

She left the plants to whoever was supposed to be looking after them and stepped out of the polytunnel. Doubt tormented her brain as she set off down the towpath.

'It's difficult. I've only seen him from the back. Now he's got dreadlocks, and it is so long ago... I'll have to find out for definite.'

As she mulled it over her thoughts became torn. She recalled the euphoria of going out with the best-looking boy in town, and the gut-wrenching feeling when he dumped her for somebody else.

'I've never really got over it ... couldn't believe it could hurt so much. It's starting again. There's nothing for it: I'll have to come back, get it out of my system,' she said with a small spring in her step and a grin on her face.

Eyeballs rolled and curtains twitched as she went by.

***

A while later the narrowboat neighbourhood watch representative reported in. He approached Robert's boat with two cans of beer held together by their original six-pack ring, and knocked on the side of the hull. Robert, who had now returned, smiled when he saw the cans.

'Welcome … a man bearing gifts. Come in. It's been a busy day.'

They went inside and Robert put another shovel of coal on the multi-fuel stove. Acrid smoke belched from the chimney as the coal struggled to ignite. They ripped open the ring pulls and watched the yellowy flame begin to dance.

'You have a secret admirer.'

'Really?' replied Robert, wondering who it could be.

'It's a she, and she was in the polytunnel an awfully long time just waiting for a glimpse of you.'

'You're winding me up.'

'Yeah. Two hours, at least. She must have been perished.'

'You can't leave it there. This she … description? Age?'

'Your age. Reasonable-looking, dressed casually … nothing else.'

'Not official, then.'

'Didn't look official. No uniform, but you never can tell. She was giving your plants a good going-over, though.'

'Oh dear, a horticulturist. Looks like I've some weeding to do.'

'Do you think she recognised the so-called *weeds*?'

'Oh, you're right, the home-grown antidepressants. I'd forgotten about them. I'd better get a move on.'

A no-news day

Emma, the *Throttle Flyer*'s latest in a line of recruits, sat at her desk idly surfing the World Wide Web.

'Just look at this,' she said, harassing her colleague who was also on his computer, and who was busily adding to a blog created by a local football manager.

'There are floods, disasters and carnage all over the world. What's going on here? Nowt,' she said with feeling.

He looked up after signing his name 'Zorro'.

'That should do it,' he added confidently, after disagreeing with everything the manager had written.

She looked over his shoulder and sneaked a look at his comment.

'Zorro,' she said, laughing.

Then, latching on to her comment, he took her to task.

'You've got to be joking… We've had floods, rescues and two murders all in the same week. How much news do you want?'

'Yeah, but that was last week. Now it's all gone cold. News moves on – it constantly needs refreshing – but here in Throttle we're back to births, deaths and marriages, and you can't invent the news, can you?'

'Oh, God, no!' They made nightmarish noises as they looked towards the wall.

A cutting pinned on the noticeboard described the

terrible, gruesome end suffered by a previous employee. Above the cutting was a stern notice reading,

Don't invent it. Look what happens if you do.

The editor, who had been listening in to the conversation, butted in.

'So … waiting for the phone to ring, are we?'

They both looked up, then nodded.

'Thought that is how it's done. Pencils at the ready,' Emma said in a slightly mocking tone.

'Whatever happened to investigative journalism?' said the editor, raising his voice.

'The same thing that has happened to the news: there is none,' shrugged Emma, not realising that the editor was getting frustrated.

Her colleague backed off when he saw the editor approaching.

'My office. Now.'

He marched her towards his almost fully glazed office, held open the door and then barked, 'Sit!'

He faced her across the desk and clenched his hands together.

'Do you like working here? Because there are plenty of people out there who would love to sit twiddling their fingers all day like you do.'

'Yeah, I like working here… I just thought it would be more exciting, that's all. Nowt goes on round here.'

'Really? Let's see, now… How can I put it so that it won't offend you?'

Fearing the worst, she sat upright.

He paused a moment.

'No, there is no other way of putting it … so here we go. You are here to report news and to put it into an interesting format that is attractive and will grab the readers' attention. With me so far?'

'Yes,' she answered.

'So far, so good. Then we put these interesting, attention-grabbing articles in the paper to attract people to buy it.' He nodded, waiting for a response. After a pause she nodded back.

'Yes,' he said, slightly louder than for normal communication.

'Yes,' she replied meekly.

'And if we sell lots of papers, advertisers will see that we are successful and popular. Don't forget the word "popular", because it is important … because if we are popular, people will want to put their adverts with us. And it's that income that pays our wages, yes?'

'Yes … popular.'

'So, if you don't go out and find some bloody news, we are all out on our arses.'

He nodded again. She nodded back. They stared at one another, as in a stalemate. Her mouth started to open, but he stopped her.

'Now go and pester that shifty estate agent. He's always up to no good.'

'What, just like that?'

'Use your feminine charm, if you have any, but don't sit here waiting for it to happen.'

He grabbed a pad and pen from his desk and thrust them at her, but she looked unsure.

'What, like a cold call? As in, "Excuse me, but are you up to anything?"'

'What's wrong with that? Ask pertinent questions and watch for body language, shifty mannerisms, a refusal to answer … that kind of thing.'

She took the pen and pad and smiled as though she

was beginning to understand.

'Look … take notes, go and rattle those cages and see if anything – er – growls. There's Joe Lagg, the estate agent. Somehow he's bound to be mixed up in the two murders.'

'Right. Two murders … mixed up,' said Emma as she scribbled.

'Then there's Roland Bullock, the landowner, who got away with murder two years ago.'

'Got away with murder…'

'Then there're the Jakeson brothers, who specialise in grievous bodily harm … though they've never been convicted, cos no one will testify in case they get beaten up.'

'Grievous bodily harm … beaten up,' she repeated.

'And then there's Fossit the farmer who, it is rumoured, has barricaded himself in the farm and is waving a double-barrelled twelve-bore shotgun about.'

'Shotgun … waving.'

'Oh, and don't forget, the murderer is still at large. He's not been caught yet. He could be hiding anywhere, right under our noses.'

Her eyes widened as she read the list back to him.

'So let me get this straight. If I tread too hard on their toes, I could easily get murdered, beaten up or shot.'

'Do it,' he said, pointing towards the door.

'Are you sure? I'm only five feet three.'

'Absolutely.'

'Can I take Zorro?' she added, pointing towards her colleague.

He did not try to understand. He just waved her goodbye.

'Go. Get out.'

The sweet aroma of old engine oil?

While Graham Fossit slept the day away Albert was dreaming dreams of old-fashioned farming. As he cleaned the plugs on the old tractor he recalled the days when farmers used to cut the grass with a huge knife called a scythe, dry the freshly cut hay in a stack called a rick, and then use enormous, lethal-looking forks to hoist the dry hay onto trailers that were usually pulled by a horse.

'Times have changed. So has the vocabulary,' he said to himself.

He had borrowed an old towel from the kitchen, and was wiping away the oil from his hands as he marvelled at the simplicity of the mechanics and wondered why the machines weren't better looked-after.

'It was all hard graft until these beauties came along,' he said to the last spark plug as he threaded it back into the engine.

He had gone all around the tractor with the now oily rag, looking for missing or broken parts, and declared that it was, 'An absolute miracle, but it seems intact.'

He dangled an old spark plug with its lead against the engine block and watched as he tentatively turned the engine over with the starting handle. It was an old mechanic's trick to tell if the electrics were working.

'Good Jesus. Nowt wrong with that,' he shouted as a

big fat blue spark generated by the magneto crackled at the end of the spark plug electrode.

'Rule number one: don't touch that,' he laughed.

Next he checked the oil using the dipstick, first wiping it clean then reinserting it to get a proper reading. He held it towards the light to observe the level of oil.

'Nowt wrong with that either,' he said with amazement.

After that, fuel was next on his list. Peering into the fuel tank, all he saw was the rusty bottom but no petrol.

'Typical: run them dry then leave them.'

After siphoning half a gallon of fuel from Graham's truck he poured it in the tractor.

'The moment of truth,' he thought as he switched everything on that he could see, then braced himself at the front of the tractor, starting handle in hand.

'Now then, no monkey business. You hear?' he said to the radiator.

When trying to start an engine with a starting handle there was always the risk that it would kick back and break the operative's thumb. His thoughts raced back almost fifty years. The tension was telling on him.

'A bit of choke, a bit of throttle – thumb well in front of the handle to prevent it being ripped off – and here we go.'

Ten minutes later, and red-faced, he sat in a sweaty heap on a bale of straw. His arm ached and his lungs seemed fit to burst.

'The frigging thing,' he muttered as he threw the starting handle to the floor.

A voice from the shadow of the barn door startled him.

'It helps if you turn the fuel tap to "petrol",' said Graham, pointing to a branch pipe on the carburettor.

'Trying to give me a heart attack, are you?' said Albert, placing a hand over his chest.

'No. It's just that it won't start on paraffin.'

'Of course. I forgot about the twin fuel system.'

They emptied the carburettor of the paraffin used for running and let in the petrol used for starting. Then Albert tried again. It started almost immediately, and settled to a tick-over.

'Bloody hell. After all these years it runs with no problem,' yelled Albert over the sound of the motor.

'No reason why not. I only used it last week,' smirked Graham. Albert did not let this small detail ruin the euphoria of the moment.

'So what are you going to do now? Play at farmers?' Graham asked cynically.

'No. We are going to play at defending the castle – or farm, if you like.'

Graham tilted his head and screwed up his eyes to indicate bewilderment.

'We are going to create a surprise for any intruder, so that we can sleep soundly at night. It shouldn't be difficult now we have this beauty,' he said, patting the radiator.

'Excellent. I am with you— oh, by the way, have you seen this?' he added, pointing to a button on the dashboard that clearly indicated the electric start.

Mucky café, dirty deeds

Despite the advice from the stranger on the plane Robin, the man from abroad (who still had a red face) had arranged a meeting with the murdering thug with the gruff voice. He was in a poor state. He had not slept since reading the article in the paper. After receiving the advice from the stranger and staying overnight in a crappy hotel he felt like death warmed up.

As he entered the café the acrid smell of old fat from the cooking of bacon and eggs made him feel sick. He was physically shaking and thought that a cup of sweet tea would calm his nerves, but any attempt to lift his cup had it dancing in his hand. Richard, who was sitting opposite, smiled, took it from him and put it back on its saucer.

'What the frig's up with you? You look like you've seen a ghost,' he grunted.

Robin tried again to hold the cup. The surface of the tea stood on end from the vibrations of his hand.

'Hang on. I'm implicated in a double murder and you say, "What's up?"'

'Keep your voice down. Now, look … the first was an accident. He just didn't get out in time. I said to him, "As soon as you see drips, get out," but he didn't.'

'What was he doing up there in the first place?'

'You don't expect me to crawl up there, do you? I'm

not built for it.' He grinned and patted his paunch.

'He was only a lad, for God's sake.'

'Ideal size. They used to send kids up chimneys, so I figured it would be OK. He should have listened.'

'What age are you living in?'

'The present, but sometimes the old ideas are the best.'

'And the second? According to the papers he was beaten to a pulp: unrecognisable,' he said, raising his voice.

'Self-defence. He came at me with a brick. What do you expect me to do? Stand there and let him hit me?' he said smugly.

'No. I expect you to kick him so hard even his mum doesn't know him.'

The thug smiled.

'He were another. I told him to shove off but he kept coming at me. If only these kids would listen...'

There was a pause as they both had a mouthful of tea.

'I sent the letters out. I cut out the letters and pasted them myself.'

'Very original. And what did it say? *Give me my money, or I will kill two people and drown the rest*?'

'Now, now, don't be ungrateful, I've done as you asked. You said, "Send out the letters. If you don't get a response, put the frighteners on them and don't leave any evidence." Well, I have, and I didn't. Well, not much,' he said, lowering his voice to a whisper.

'You've done that, all right. The entire frigging town is terrified.'

'Apart from one, that is.'

'One what?'

'One bit of the plan that could catch us out.'

'I don't like the way you keep referring to "us". It was

you who killed them, remember?'

The thug's face was gripped with anger.

'You can't opt out you little shit. Let me tell you, if you don't put the other half of the money in my hand, I will see to it that you get implicated for the lot. OK?'

'OK, OK. The first half you've got. You'll get the second half when we sort this out. Now who or what is this glitch in the plan?'

He was just about to speak when the waitress came to the table holding a cloth. She looked down at the puddles of tea, then at him. She did not hesitate, but lifted his cup and saucer and wiped away the mess.

'Like another one, would you?' she said in a couldn't-care-less way. 'Bit stronger this time?' she added.

'Yes, OK. Good idea.'

The waitress wandered off with the order and Robin waited till she was out of earshot.

'Go on. Go on, tell me about the glitch.'

The thug braced himself for what he knew would be a bollocking.

'The farmer – the one whose field I dug up, just as you said...'

'Yes, yes. Go on.'

'I've still got the sketch you gave me. It showed me exactly where to dig the ditch.'

'Get on with it.'

'Well, he knows me. I had to pay him. We might have to pay him a visit and pay him some more.'

'Did you tell him your name?'

'No, but he would recognise me.'

Robin sank in his seat and put his head in his hands.

'Are we going to kick the shit out of him?'

'No. Just a quiet word, then we will kick the shit out of

him if he can't keep his gob shut.'

'Just a point … are you sure there's no evidence? You didn't leave anything behind, did you?'

'Such as?'

'Oh, I don't know. Tools, equipment … anything like that.'

'No.'

'The digger you used … where did you leave it? Did you take it back to the hire people? What about the hire agreement? It's got your name on it. Where is it?'

The thug looked confused. He stared at the ceiling, mouthed as though he was counting back the days, then said, 'Frig. It's in the back of the digger.'

'So where did you leave it?'

'At the farm.'

'So when I asked you, literally seconds ago, "Have you left any evidence?" and you said, "No," you hadn't taken into account an enormous great digger?'

'I forgot.'

'You forgot. How can you forget a bleeding great thing like that?'

He shrugged his shoulders and offered an inane smile.

'He's either stupid or mad or insane, or all three,' Robin thought.

The waitress brought his tea and slid the bill under the sugar bowl. He thanked her, then wondered about the thought of drinking the dark substance in the cup – and the means of implicating the thug for the lot.

As he sat opposite him, Richard the psychopath also harboured thoughts of an exit strategy but, as per his line of work, it was more grisly.

'I could dump him at the police station entrance with a note nailed to his head saying, *It was me who did it.*

Momentarily they were both lost in their thoughts. Robin considered that he had the makings of a plan of escape, so he sipped the tea, grimaced and spoke.

'Then that's two reasons to go back to the farm.'

The thug came back from his daydream about nail guns and agreed.

'Sounds good to me,' he said.

Plan of action? The *Throttle Flyer* press room

Emma and her colleague Gareth sat at their desks. They were mulling over the prospect of approaching and asking pertinent questions of homicidal maniacs in order to have something to report and, as a consequence, an article to print.

'When I joined this paper they said nothing about approaching murderers or prospective murderers about their alibis or intentions. I'm only on a mangy pittance, and they want me to put my life on the line just to sell soddin' papers. Well, they can bog off. They can stuff their job where the sun doesn't shine.'

Gareth grinned.

'Got another job to go to, have you? Seen the limited list in the small ads? Fancy stacking shelves, do you?'

Then, without taking his eyes away from the computer screen, he offered support to her argument and an insight into the world of espionage.

'Don't be too hasty. Jobs aren't that easy to come by. Besides, there's more than one way to kill a pig … other than shoving strawberries up its arse.'

Emma screwed up her face.

'You've been living here too long if you're coming out with statements like that. It's time you got away from this so-called millstone grit.'

'You know what I mean. You don't have to confront them. What we have to do is a bit of fishing ... We need to delve, and stir the muddy pool that is the happenings in Throttle.'

Gareth became all theatrical, and demonstrated stirring by twirling a pencil round in a paper cup and gritting his teeth.

Emma smiled. 'You should be on stage.'

They sat back for a moment. Then, not wanting to dampen his enthusiasm, Emma raised the question, 'OK, but how?'

'A stake-out,' he announced. 'Dah, de dah dah,' he sang to the signature tune of *The Sweeney*.

She looked at him as though he had flipped.

Gareth offered what he thought was clarification.

'It was probably a bit before your time, but *The Sweeney* – short for Sweeney Todd, a barber who murdered his customers – is rhyming slang for the flying squad. Anyway, they always had stake-outs – and we'll need a flask, binoculars and probably warm coats.'

She still looked confused.

'I just don't fancy this standing around waiting, especially round here. You'd get reported, ironically.'

She swung round on her chair and fired up the computer, then rattled the keys of the keyboard until she found an answer to their quandary.

'It might have been OK ages ago, but now you can do it from the comfort of your living room.'

'For those who are fortunate to have living rooms,' he muttered.

'OK ... from the comfort of a bedsit.'

'Sorry. Continue.'

'If we go on t'Internet we can pick up bugs for next to

nowt, long-lens cameras and…'

'Long macs and dark glasses,' he smirked.

'You are not taking this seriously. Here I am trying to get you out of the office and away from the claws of the boss, and all you can do is take the piss.'

There was a moment's silence as they both thought out their next move.

'All right. Truce,' he said.

He nodded and smiled but remained silent. Emma, feeling she had gone too far, asked a question.

'You know when they said it is now a metaphorical hanging offence to invent the news?'

'I think I do.'

'Well we know that Roland Bullock was guilty, and he probably paid good money to a barrister to get him off.'

'Y-e-s.' He dragged out the word to let her know he had doubts.

'Then can we not invent the evidence to convict him, get a good story and a bonus?'

He stood up.

'I'm off. It's called perverting evidence and wasting police time. They lock you up for an awfully long time and close down the paper.'

She grabbed the edge of his jacket.

'All right. We'll do it your way, but it sounds boring.'

'It might be boring, but it's legal.'

***

Gareth got in early the next day and waited for his boss to arrive. As he entered the building he followed him into his office. He stood waiting as he took off his coat and sat at his desk.

'Yes? What is it now?' he asked impatiently.

'You know these psychopaths you want us to question?'

'Psychopaths? What psychopaths?'

'Well, all right. Murderers, possibly double murderers.'

'OK. Go on, then.'

'You wouldn't want us to get hurt or anything. After all, you would never sleep if anything happened to us … would you?'

'Hurry up. I haven't got all day.'

'We need these bugs so we can listen without getting our faces altered.'

Gareth handed him a computer printout showing all manner of covert bugging equipment.

The editor began to mumble about the rules of journalism. 'We never had these in my day. It comes under phone tapping and listening devices. I think the bottom line is that we think it's OK to do, so long as you don't get caught. If you do get caught, we disown you and throw you to the wolves. Got it?'

'So I can go and buy them, then?'

'I suppose so, but use petty cash … no receipt.'

Later that afternoon Gareth arrived back at the office with a large carrier bag. He unpacked the cardboard boxes then displayed the contents on the desk.

'Have you seen these?' he said as he passed two multi-socket units across the table.

'Yes, OK … two multi-sockets.'

'No. Well, yes. They still work as multi-sockets.'

'Go on, then. What are they? Are you telling me that they look like multi-sockets but in fact they are something entirely different?'

'Yes,' he said happily. 'These are going to make discreet surveillance easy. These are the latest, up-to-the-minute listening devices.'

'These are multi-sockets,' she said, picking one up and spinning it in her hand.

'Hey,' he shouted. 'Careful. They're not cheap.' He leant forward and whispered surreptitiously behind his hand. 'And, I might say, they're illegal.'

'What can be illegal about two multi-sockets?'

'You don't understand, do you? These may look like multi-sockets, but inside is a receiver and a transmitter.'

'What, in here?' she queried, putting her eye close to it.

'It still works as a socket, so all you ... all *we* have to do is to fit this into the mains socket and – Bob's your uncle – we can listen in on these.' He dangled a pair of headphones, then put them on to demonstrate. 'You can hear what people are saying through these.'

'I know how they work, divvy. So what's the transmission distance?' asked Emma.

'Oh, getting all technical now, aren't we?'

'We need to know,' she added as she read the instructions on the box.

'A hundred metres – as long as there's nothing big in the way, such as a house or a car. What do they mean by "big"?'

'We'll have to have a practice at what a hundred metres looks like, or we could be there all day thinking they've said nothing.'

'Excited, aren't you? This reporter business ... it's all gone James Bond,' said Gareth, with obvious delight in his voice. 'So we'll do the estate agent's first, and then the site office.' Then he took a breather as another problem got in the way. 'Don't exactly know how, mind you. We might have to break in ... crowbars and torches in the dark of the night. Splintered doorways could raise suspicion.'

She looked at him, exasperated.

'You haven't got a clue, have you? One minute you're talking about it being legal or not. The next you want to smash your way into the office. Get real.'

'OK, Mrs Clever Clogs. Got any suggestions?'

'It's easy. I distract them while you fit the plug.'

'Subterfuge,' replied Gareth.

'Call it what you want. It's better than your way. Now then, we need a story – one that will appear real and appropriate.'

They practised the script in the office, then paced out one hundred metres.

***

Outside the estate agent's they went over their lines again.

'Don't forget to follow the script and play the part,' she instructed.

'Feels awkward ... I've never been married before.' They each took a deep breath and went in. Gareth lagged behind.

'Come on,' she hissed, pulling at his coat.

'Can I help you?' said the secretary as she rose from her desk.

'Well ... er, yes. We are looking for a house,' they said in unison.

'Well, you are in the right place. This *is* an estate agent's,' she replied haughtily.

She looked them up and down. Then, having assessed their appearance and behaviour, she used her experience as a judge of character and potential income.

'What type of house are you looking for? Pre-war

semi, or terraced?'

'Detached,' Gareth blurted out.

'Price range?'

'Oh, half a million,' he said with a swagger.

Emma backed away, embarrassed.

'Take no notice. He's just a little nervous,' she said as she faced the lady.

'You're ruining this,' she said, and turned to face Gareth.

'A nice little terraced cottage will do, with at least three bedrooms,' she said as she looked down and sheepishly patted her stomach.

'Oh, I see. Well, we have a nice selection over here,' said the secretary. Emma followed her to the bargain corner.

'Feel free to browse,' said the lady, and curled her top lip.

They looked around at the sale boards while at the same time looking for a mains socket.

'The only one I've seen is powering the computer,' whispered Gareth.

'So be it,' said Emma as she rummaged in her handbag for the adaptor.

'Give it here. Now you distract her while I do the deed.'

Emma looked around. In an effort to get the lady to face away from the socket she had to divert her view.

'Hello … er, this one looks nice. Can we have the sheet for it?' Emma pointed towards the photo of a farm with outbuildings, ten acres of land and a price tag of £800,000.

'I thought you were looking for a terraced house,' added the secretary as she flicked through the file of houses for sale.

'Got to keep your options open. You never know ... I could win the lottery.' Emma moved round to face the lady while Gareth quickly got on his knees and inserted the adaptor between the computer plug and the wall socket. Seconds later he was back looking at a house he could not afford.

'This one looks nice—' he said.

'Well, thanks. Got to be going ... other houses to see,' said Emma, interrupting him.

'Yes ... a big farm to see. Might just be within our budget.'

'Oh, OK,' said the lady, shocked at their hurry to leave. It was then that she spotted the blank computer screen.

'What's happened here? What have you done? I was in the middle of a big document. I'll have to start all over again,' she shrieked.

'Power loss. Happens all the time round here ... you should always back up your work,' Gareth shouted as the door closed behind them.

They hurriedly walked down the street and tried to appear as though they were not hurrying.

'That was close. I'm sure she spotted me messing with the plug,' Gareth said, still facing down the street.

'Half a million? Are you mad? You made her suspicious right away. Anyway, let's have some coffee first – my nerves are jangling – and then we'll do the next one.'

Gareth nodded, and held out his hand. It was shaking.

'Good fun, though, eh?' he laughed.

'Oh, aye – if you're into heart attacks.'

They went further down the street to the newly opened Italian café. They sat on a cosy leather sofa and kept staring at each other and exhaling until they calmed down. Following a double espresso, they each took a deep breath and set off for the site office of the new estate.

'Come on, then. Let's do it,' said Gareth, winding her up.

'We'll do the same as in the estate agent's. Keep calm, wait for your moment ... then, as I keep them distracted, do it. But no stupid comments,' said Emma confidently.

'And if I get it wrong I get my face rearranged. No pressure there, then,' said Gareth.

They stood outside the site office. Gareth knocked on the door, then hastily stood behind her. Before she could move, the door opened.

'What?' grunted Simon, his large bulk filling the frame of the doorway.

Gareth and Emma stepped back and looked up. They had been expecting a little less hostility, but carried on regardless.

'We are looking for a house. We've just come from the estate agent's, and they sent us round here for a look.'

Simon didn't move.

'Can we have a look at the plan? Only we need a nice garden for the kids?' said Emma, feigning a maternal tone.

'It's the same as in the estate agent's. Besides ... it's not the way it's done,' Simon replied gruffly.

'She said yours would be better, neater and more up to date,' added Emma, trying to flatter him.

'She?'

'The woman in the estate agent's ... she said that because you are on site it would be bang up to date. Can we have a look?'

'This is a work cabin, not a sales point. Health and

safety, considerate construction, hard hats, the smell of drying plaster and wet cement… Not a sales office … get it?'

'Go on,' pleaded Emma. 'Just a quick look. We are getting married soon, and we need a house in a hurry.'

Gareth flinched as she grabbed his arm, put it round her, beamed up at him then patted her stomach.

'Like that, is it?' said Simon, winking at Gareth. Before he had a chance to think and possibly deny the situation, Simon softened. 'Go on, then, but only a quick look.'

On the way across the office Gareth had to walk around the newly installed evidence board. He stopped, stared at the cartoons, smiled and carried on. His eyes darted round the site hut. There was no computer, just a brew station.

'It'll have to do,' he thought.

Meanwhile Emma kept Simon busy with a barrage of questions as Gareth inserted the multi-socket between the kettle plug and the wall socket. While trying not to fumble or make a noise he pulled out the kettle plug and slotted in the multi-socket, then furtively slid behind Simon and Emma.

'OK. We've seen all we need to see,' he shouted.

Simon was just about to answer Emma's latest question about the thickness of the loft insulation when she cut him short.

'Thanks. Bye … it's been lovely. It really has.'

'Yes … thanks for the info. It's been very useful,' added Gareth. He was trying to sound convincing, but actually sounded wooden.

As they left they had to push past Reginald, who was entering the hut.

'Going on?' he grunted as he turned to watch them

leave.

'She's up the duff and needs a house in a hurry. They said they were sent by Lagg's woman for a look around,' Simon explained.

'That's not the way it's done, not after all that's happened here,' barked Reginald.

'I said that, but … they … appeared … genuine…' Simon hesitated, as though cogs were slowly turning in his brain.

'Make me a brew,' barked Reginald as he picked up the phone.

A few moments later he said, 'No, she didn't. Where's my brew?'

Simon looked blank.

'She didn't send them, and where's my brew?' Reginald repeated grumpily. He looked at the kettle. The small light indicating power on, was off.

'It helps if you switch it on,' he shouted.

'Spooky,' said Simon, rolling his eyes.

'Go on then, get it over with … another of your soddin' psychic observations.'

Simon stared at the kettle.

'I didn't turn off the socket … you didn't turn off the socket… It never gets turned off… They weren't sent by Lagg's woman and, chances are, they're not getting married.'

'Well, I smell a rat. Anyway, how do you know they were not going to get married?'

'I could see it in her eyes. She were all false.'

Thinking they had got away with it, the two reporters tentatively held hands and walked briskly along the unmade roads.

'As before, best foot forward and keep looking straight

ahead,' instructed Gareth as they splashed through the building site mud towards the exit.

Moments later, having got their breath back, they listened in … but were disappointed to hear nothing at all.

***

In the hut Simon and Reginald sat in silence. They stared at their mugs of tea then at the evidence board. A feeling of doubt had crept over them. Then Reginald offered a sobering thought.

'We haven't cocked it up again, just as the houses are about to be finished, have we?'

Simon added his words of wisdom.

'When it were small – the business, that is – it were easy. Do a job, lie about the quote, ask for more, threaten them if they didn't come up with the cash… Easy. It's too complicated now. We've lost control. Contracts, plans, labour, dealing with foreigners…'

'What did you say?' said Reginald, as he sat upright.

'Contracts?'

'No, at the end.'

'Dealing with foreigners.'

'Grab your mac,' shouted Reginald as he slapped down his mug and spilt his tea.

'Is it raining?' said Simon, looking skyward.

Reginald grabbed the keys to the van, rushed towards the door and said, 'Come on. I think I've sussed it.'

They climbed into the van, which resembled the inside of a builder's hut, and set off. As they drove Reginald beamed, and Simon put on the usual puzzled expression.

***

Round the corner from the site entrance, Gareth and Emma watched the van drive away.

'We've probably got half an hour. It's illegal, dangerous … and if we get caught… Crikey, I daren't think. But there are answers in the hut, I'm sure of it,' proposed Gareth.

Emma shook her head in disbelief.

'Oh … go on, then. But we'll have to be quick. Just one point … what exactly are we looking for?'

'I'm not sure … some kind of evidence that could implicate them in the murders. Oh, I don't know – but it's an opportunity not to be missed, and we know they're going to be gone a while.'

'Oh, great. We could be put away behind bars for no reason: facial disfigurement at no extra charge.'

'Come on, hurry up.'

***

After trawling the streets of a similar village to Throttle for what seemed ages, Reginald and Simon arrived at another building site. The evening gloom had descended and, with the absence of streetlights, dark meant proper dark. They trudged past the show house, which was emblazoned with bunting and adverts advising the many methods of financing a new home and relieving you of your savings.

'Strange, really,' said Simon as he stared at the massive advert with a picture of a family beaming from ear to ear.

'What is?'

'They've just saddled themselves with thousands of pounds worth of debt, and they're happy.'

'Takes all sorts,' replied Reginald as he squinted into the distance.

'What we looking for? It's pitch black,' Simon asked

breathlessly as the pace speeded up.

'You'll see.'

They continued wandering around the unfinished houses, ankle-deep in mud and builders' rubble. As they went further on, the unmade roads began to look like farm tracks. There were some wooden crosses at intervals to indicate that one day these would be dream homes. Simon was now completely puzzled, as Reginald walked to where foundations had only just been laid. The majority of the builders had gone home long ago, but Reginald was looking for a different kind of community. A noise alerted him. He turned round. The sound of a generator pointed him towards a large, almost complete house on the edge of the site.

'Bingo. Come on,' he urged.

They moved quietly towards the house. The roof was nearly finished and the windows and doors had temporary sheets of plywood nailed on for security. A chink of light coming from a doorway gave away the fact that the house was occupied.

As they moved closer the laughter of foreign voices and the clatter of domesticity could be heard. Reginald pointed to the front doorway. They clambered over bricks and scaffolding poles then knocked lightly on the plywood sheet propped against the doorjamb. The voices and the noise of the radio stopped abruptly. Then the lights went out. Minutes later a dark-faced man peered from round the side of the house. Reginald moved closer to be able to see the man's features.

'What want?' he growled in broken English.

'It's OK. We're not official or anything. We're just looking for someone – a friend – and were wondering if he is here.'

'What want?' he repeated, this time with an added growl.

Reginald smiled at the man to calm him, and asked, 'Is Urinal in here?'

'Urinal?' queried Simon quietly.

'Shut up,' Reginald hissed.

He repeated more slowly to the man of few words, 'Is Urinal in here? Does he live here? Only … we would like a word.'

The man did not answer but smiled through a mouth full of bad teeth, then held up a finger to indicate that he partly understood.

'I'll be back,' he said in a throaty voice.

They looked at one another then Reginald realised.

'He's learnt his English from watching *The Terminator*,' he said, and shook his head.

Simon shook his head and moved closer.

'What are we doing here, and who is Urinal? You bring me to the weirdest places.'

The man went inside and imparted the message as best he could. Minutes later another man with slightly better teeth and a greater vocabulary returned.

'Reggie,' he grinned.

'Urinal,' Reginald replied, as though to a long-lost friend.

'You come in, but be careful. We leave it rough to keep people away,' he advised with a slight Eastern European accent.

He waved to them to come forward. They followed him round the back and in through the previously boarded-up kitchen door. Once inside the soon-to-be-completed detached executive home took on the appearance of a hostel housing four or five men. Some were cooking or watching TV, while another came down the unpainted central staircase in a towelling robe. He had just had a shower in the unfinished en suite marble bathroom. Reginald soon recognised them, and waved. This was the sum total of communication.

It was at this moment that Simon put two and two together, and a dim light came on in his head.

'They are plumbers. Urinal … I get it now. Why didn't you say? Is there one called "Shower tray"?'

Reginald sighed.

'Just shut up and do as he says.'

Urinal pointed towards a large settee.

'Please … sit.'

'Very nice,' added Reginald as he patted the cushion.

'You have very good charity shops in England. We get clothing and furniture for next to nothing – and now you have food banks, so we eat for free. We like it very much here.'

There was a pause, then he added, 'So … rumour has it that all our good work is for nothing. We worked very hard to get the job done. Now it has to be done again.'

'Well, not quite. We caught it before it did too much damage. There are a few knackered carpets, that's all. Dehumidifiers will take care of the rest, and the stains will be covered with emulsion,' said Reginald, putting on a brave face.

'You always did have an answer, I remember. Any problem … go see Reggie. We enjoyed working for you. We had a very nice house on your site.'

'Did you? We never knew, did we, Simon? Anyway … the reason we're here, though, is that we don't know all the answers. It's who and why that are the issue. Who did it, and why?' he pleaded.

'You don't know? I thought you knew everything. Mr Robin is the who, and the why is probably because he has not been paid. He can get very upset when he is not paid. We have finished on your site, and he has not been paid. That is very bad. No wonder he is angry. He has men who collect the debts … maybe it was one of them who flooded the houses.'

'Mr Robin … is that his real name? Only we have been told to go and find out who he is so that we can put matters straight. We can't do that unless we know who we are dealing with, can we?'

'Mr Robin … we call him Mr Robin Bastard. That's all we know. Two years ago you or your boss must have spoken to him. He is the one who gets us the work. We are cheaper than UK men, but you pay him a one-off fee for no questions asked.' He smiled, held out his palms and added, 'And as you can see, we live rent-free and tax-free, and we are much cheaper than your people.'

Reginald turned to Simon, who just shrugged his shoulders and shook his head.

'I think he dealt with a Mr Ballcock,' added Urinal.

They shook their heads again.

'Nobody we know,' Reginald said.

'The kettle's just boiled. Cup of sweet tea and biscuits? Sell-by date just gone, but still OK.'

'Yes, please,' replied Simon.

'Very civilised. You seem to have it sorted here. It seems a shame that the houses have to be finished and sold.'

'It's OK, but we have to keep moving on. We don't want anyone to get too friendly, otherwise we have less money to send home.'

Reginald nodded knowingly as he took hold of his

mug of tea, then mouthed the word 'tax' to Simon.

They were just about to leave when they noticed the other men sniggering in their native language.

'Oh … something funny?' snarled Simon.

'I'm sorry. They mean no harm. It's just that they are curious about your clothing … it's a bit strange: you in black, your brother in white.'

'Just a difference of opinion, that's all,' explained Simon. 'We are sleuths: temporary detectives. I say they have white macs, but my brother here says they wear donkey jackets.'

Urinal interpreted for the non-English-speaking by including the noise of a baying donkey. The laughter became uncontrollable.

They walked back to the van with their pride a little dented, so as they climbed in they threw the jacket and the mackintosh in the back.

'That's it, we'll go incognito from now on … blend into the background, hide in doorways and shadows. We might have to get some camouflage clothing. They had some in the charity shop,' Simon suggested.

'No,' Reginald said firmly as he fired up the Transit.

As they drove off with the wheels spinning in the mud they looked around the building site, and could swear they saw other houses with chinks of light coming from the gaps in boarded-up windows.

'Brickies, roofers, joiners … they all need a place to stay,' Reginald reasoned.

'Electricians, gas fitters, carpet fitters, glaziers, plasterers, decorators, kitchen fitters… How come we don't have a nice house?' Simon went on.

Meanwhile, back at the site hut, nerves were beginning

to get edgy. They had sifted through the mountain of documentation and plans located in the cupboard, but nothing had alerted them to any criminality.

'This is hopeless,' Emma said as she pointed the torch at her wrist.

'Time's up. The clock has beaten you, so let's beat it before they beat us… Do you like that?'

'Yes, very funny. But this is our last opportunity to poke around here. If we don't find anything we have to stand on street corners with headphones on, which would be a serious credibility issue.'

Gareth had been rummaging through the unopened mail in a cardboard box on top of the desk. His increasing urgency had overtaken his ability to be tidy.

'If you really want to give the game away then just carry on throwing things about. Put stuff back where you found it. They might be idiots, but they're not daft.'

Gareth peeked inside a large envelope, then reached further inside. As he saw the contents his heart began to thump.

'Hey … bingo. Look at this.'

He pulled out a large envelope. Inside was a sheet with letters cut out of newspapers glued to it.

'Look at this. If this isn't a threatening letter, I don't know what is.'

Emma looked at her watch again.

'Come on, hurry up – unless you fancy looking like Quasimodo.'

'Coming, coming…'

As he hurriedly stuffed the envelope inside his jacket, one of the letters cut from a newspaper gently floated to the floor.

'What about this?'

He pointed to the cardboard box that was strewn with opened letters and ripped paper.

'There's no time for that now. It'll match the rest of the office. Come on, will you?' Emma hissed, getting angry.

The following morning Simon was first in and put on the kettle. He was studying the information board when Reginald arrived. As he turned towards him they both spotted the letter cut out of a newspaper on the floor. Reginald picked it up and noticed the other letters littering his desk. He looked at Simon accusingly, who instinctively raised his hands.

'Hey … not me your honour. Been nowhere near.'

'Then you'd better add some additional info to your board.'

They completed their everyday chores then settled for a mid-morning brew. As they stared through the window over a cup of tea, they watched builders go from house to house with pumps and dehumidifiers in an attempt to dry out the properties. They analysed the situation.

'According to Urinal, somebody has failed to pay somebody else for something. We don't know what, but whatever it was, it was worth killing for, and somebody else was willing to break into our hut to find out.'

His thoughts went round like a record.

'So, we have Urinal telling us that a Mr Ballcock failed to pay a Mr Robin, and as a result our houses were flooded by Big Dick – or, as he prefers to be called, Large Richard… So we know who did it. So who are the others with an interest in our affairs?'

Reginald looked at Simon for a response. Simon, though, appeared to be in a trance.

'Hello. Is there anybody there?'

'I was just putting my thoughts together. Over the past few days it's been weird, what with the water and the deaths and things. And there's something else.'

He rolled his eyes towards the wall, then up to the ceiling, then down into the corner of the hut and pointed to the kettle.

'Something very strange is going on.'

He pointed again at the kettle.

'I'm in charge of brewing up. Yes?'

Reginald nodded exaggeratedly in an effort to speed things up.

'Yes. Come on, will you?'

'That's my space, my kettle, my tea bags and my sour milk. Yes?'

Reginald nodded again, but then lost it, and asked, 'What's the problem?'

Simon rose from his chair and walked quietly towards the brew area. He looked under the brew table and pointed towards the multi-socket, from which a short thin black wire dangled.

'It wasn't there the other day. I would know, cos I'm the brew person.'

Reginald moved closer to inspect the socket.

'Oh, dear,' he said as he wondered what was going on.

He put his index finger to his lips, crooked it then pointed to the door. Moments later, outside, they spoke in hushed tones.

'Who the hell wants to bug us?'

Simon smiled and tapped his nose.

'Shall we find out?'

***

That evening they sat in the hut close to the socket, each with a hastily scribbled script.

Simon nodded towards Reginald to start the performance.

'So, Simon ... now that we know who did the murders, what are we going to do?'

'Well, Reginald, I think that we should write out a letter complete with all the facts and put it in an envelope in your top drawer and leave it till tomorrow ... and then we will post it.'

'Now then ... let's lock up, have an early night and go for a pint.'

'An excellent idea... Let us go.'

For extra realism they added the sound of the door being shut and locked before they sat on the floor in the darkness. The silent order was too much for one brother to bear.

'I could do with a brew,' added Simon.

Reginald scowled and put his finger to his lips.

***

They didn't have long before the door slowly opened.

'I could have sworn I heard them lock the door as they left,' whispered Emma.

Moonlight filled the hut as the door fully opened. They entered, then Reginald kicked it shut. Screams and bad language filled the hut till Simon put on the light and stood against the door.

'You're going nowhere, you two,' he shouted.

After a momentary lapse in conversation, Reginald took the initiative.

'So what is it you want? What makes you want to bug our hut, then break in?'

'Clues, that's all. Two murders, a flood … and now it's gone cold. Everyone is carrying on as though nothing's happened. The police haven't come up with anything–'

'So you thought we would know. Is that it?' interjected Reginald.

'Well, it is your houses that were affected. The water went straight to them.'

Then Gareth pushed his luck. He pointed his finger at Simon and threatened him. Almost instantly he wished he hadn't.

'You have upset someone. A nutter, by all accounts.'

Simon went for him, grabbed him by the throat and pinned him to the door. He saw the fear in Gareth's face and moved closer, almost touching nose to nose.

'We are simple folk who are just trying to earn an honest living. We don't murder or get involved in murder – a bit of GBH, maybe, but not murder. And if we knew who had flooded our beautiful houses, do you not think we would have practised a bit of GBH by now?'

Gareth nodded.

'OK. Now then, hand over the gadget that goes with this.' Simon held out the multi-socket.

Gareth rummaged in his pocket for the headphones.

'Here, you can have them.'

'Good boy. Now then, let's see: breaking and entering, police, loss of job, jobs are hard to come by round here, reputation up the spout, headlines in your own newspaper… That would be something, eh… Or you can do us a little favour. What's it to be?'

Horrified, Gareth and Emma looked at one another.

'Favour … what kind of favour?'

'Simple. It's what you are good at. All you have to do is, like before, pretend to be a couple looking for a house.

Go to this building site and find this house.'

Reginald held out a scrap of paper with the details on.

'Say you are interested in this particular one, and can you have a quick look round?'

He then handed back the bug.

'Then leave your gadget on a shelf or in a plug or something. Use your head. Of course, if you don't…' he added

'Yes, yes, all right. We get the message,' replied Emma, getting tetchy.

'But do it soon or GBH will come looking, and we know where you live.'

Outside Emma shook with horror, but Gareth smirked.

'We've still got one in the other office – and we can also listen in on what's said on the building site, which kills two birds with one stone. We get to hear what's going on at the sharp end. Then if we're quick we hear the response, and we've got away with our faces intact.'

'You don't mind if I don't share your enthusiasm,' said Emma weakly.

***

As instructed, Emma and Gareth presented themselves at the site office. Reginald had used this as a point of reference. With their backs to the site office they held out the location details and rotated them to get the correct orientation. This activity alerted a salesman in the show house to a potential customer. While thinking about his month-end total, he grabbed his clipboard, a brochure, applied a smile and marched out.

'Lovely day. Can I help you?' asked the man in a suit, who was now wearing a white hard hat.

Emma, eager to show willing, jumped in.

'Er, we are getting married shortly, and – er – we would like to see this particular house. We have been told it is ideal for our family circumstances.' She looked down at her flat stomach, expanded it and patted her raised abdomen.

'Oh. OK, let me see,' said the man as he took hold of the information. He looked at the scrap of paper then back at his list then back to Emma's stomach, which had flattened again.

'Sorry, but this house is out of bounds to the public because of health and safety. It's not finished. You wouldn't be able to see anything, anyway. It's just a pile of bricks and mortar at present… You can see it on this plan here … or come back in about six weeks.'

Emma put on her most sorrowful expression.

'Are you sure? We have a friend who told us about this particular house. He said it has everything a growing family would need. We have come a long way … only we would like to see the extent of the garden for the children, and which way it faces the sun … only we are keen gardeners, and have ideas on being self-sufficient. You know, growing our own veg an' stuff.'

The man ushered Emma into his office. He passed her a glossy brochure.

'It's all in here. Also … you can see all you need on here,' he said, pointing to a wallchart. 'This arrow indicates north, and this box indicates the size of the floor plan. You don't need to see the house.'

'So you are not going to let us in, then?' she said, loud enough for Gareth to hear.

'Sorry. No,' he apologised.

'So how many bathrooms does it have, and what size

are the bedrooms? Can we choose our own tiles?' she rambled on, trying to gain more time.

'Sorry, Miss – er, Mrs – it's all in here,' he added, passing her another brochure and sensing a sales failure.

Meanwhile Gareth was standing outside, and as he heard Emma quiz the man further he twigged to what she was trying to do. He looked around, and spotted what he thought was the house from the description:

One detached house on the edge of the site, part-built

He ran through the mud over to the only house that fitted the description. After stopping at the front he was puzzled by the fact that all the doors and windows were boarded over. Then a man came out from behind the house and walked along the edge of the site. He did not notice Gareth standing there.

'That's it,' he said to himself.

He stepped down off what eventually would be a gravel drive with a privet hedge and set off round the back. His luck was in. The man had left the plywood door ajar. His mind raced.

'If he's left it open he must be coming back,' he thought. On stepping quietly into what would be the kitchen, he heard foreign voices. His heart started to thump: he had relied on there not being anyone else in. Quickly he took the multi-socket listening device and placed it in the socket behind a microwave oven on a makeshift shelf. As he nervously stepped back out he heard more foreign voices coming his way. However, on looking down he spotted a discarded hard hat.

'Don't panic,' he thought. With his collar up and the hard hat pulled firmly down, he marched purposefully past the gang of workmen arriving for their mid-morning tea break. He nodded and smiled, while at the same time trying to hide his face. Once outside he found it difficult not to break into a run. Nervous sweat trickled down his neck as he related the story to Emma.

'It was close, very close. I don't want many more like that ... but I couldn't understand a word, couldn't put my finger on the language. I don't know what the heavy mob are going to get out of it.'

'Did you do the deed, though?'

'Yeah. Oh, yeah ... but one thing crossed my mind as I scarpered from the house. From what I've read, these guys think life is cheap – you know, a life means nothing. And – let's face it – a building site is an ideal place to get rid of a corpse ... if I had got caught ... if you know what I mean.'

'You're not sniggering now, are you? You were lucky this time. I heard they carry big knives. Sleep tight, and don't let the memories bite,' she mocked as she wiped a finger across her neck in a throat-slitting gesture.

'Thanks for the support,' Gareth said with a wan smile.

Team meeting, *Throttle Flyer*

The editor looked out from his office window. Normally banter would flow between the two wily reporters. However, the past couple of days had been a bit of a shock to their carefree lives. Both sat thoughtfully at their desks. A bit bemused by the scene, the editor rose from his desk and decided to find out what was going on. 'OK. In here, you two. Let's have today's plan of action.' They entered quietly and stood in front of his desk as though they were being disciplined.

'Ooh ... what's going on here, then? Had a fall-out, have we? Not the usual hyperactive, go-getting, bubbly reporters?'

'We've had a funny twenty-four hours.'

'Nearly got us killed,' bawled Emma.

'We didn't,' hissed Gareth.

'OK, OK. Emma, what happened?'

'A lot of shady business. We put a bug in the estate agent's ... we've not got anything from there, just a load of everyday chitchat. We put one in the site hut, but they spotted it and trapped us into going back.'

A tear rolled down Emma's cheek.

'Keep calm. You're safe now ... what happened next?' he asked, eager to know but at the same time offering a modicum of concern.

'Then the two nutters who run the building site

threatened us. They said that if we didn't put a bug on another building site they would put us in hospital.'

'Go on,' said the editor, rubbing his hands.

'Then he—' she said, pointing to Gareth, 'he was nearly caught by a load of foreign workers when he was putting the bug in the house.' She wiped her eyes and carried on.

'And by the look of them they wouldn't think twice about putting us in with the foundations. I tell you, it was so close.'

The editor smiled.

'Welcome to the world of undercover reporting. You'll get used to it. So what's the next move? It looks to me that you have touched a very raw nerve.'

'No support, no sympathy, no extra money … you want us to go out again and risk a beating?'

'Haven't you heard of the term "paparazzo"? Then let me educate you. These reporters hide in doorways, take a bit of risk, report wrongs, solve crimes, and take photos of celebs in compromising positions – but, more to the point – make headlines and sell papers. This is your opportunity to get a scoop. It's what all reporters dream of, and it's on your doorstep.'

'Really? So all reporters dream of being this far from a beating?' Emma indicated a slim gap between her finger and thumb.

'Sit down.'

The editor sensed fear in his staff. He understood the anxiety of chasing a story – he had experienced it himself when he was a reporter. However, in the back of his mind he knew they were on to something and he did not want to let them talk themselves into quitting.

'I think you are on to something big here, something

that could be the making of you. When you move on from here, and you will, you will always be able to say to the next editor, "It was me who broke the story." That is, when you crack it.'

Out of sight and undercover

The following evening Reginald and Simon parked their van close to but out of sight of the unfinished but occupied house. Meanwhile – unbeknown to them – Gareth and Emma were also at the site, and were sitting in one of the rooms of an unfinished house round the corner. Emma and Simon both complained of the cold.

Gareth tried to lighten the atmosphere with an observation.

'Catch me buying one of these? It's bloody freezing in here, and it stinks something God-awful.'

'Sewage, or something,' added Emma.

After about an hour, and just before both parties were about to give up, a muddied four-by-four splashed through the puddles and stopped outside the house.

Headlights dimmed, the driver slammed the car door shut, then – without knocking – went inside. He went straight into the living area. Because he was a big man he had to duck under the string of temporary lights. The occupants recognised him immediately, and almost stood to attention. They let him speak first.

'All OK?'

'*Si, ja, tak,*' the group nodded.

'That's very good,' he said with a strange grin, but then his mood changed.

He turned and faced Urinal and asked, with slight

menace in his voice, 'Any unwanted visitors? Anyone been poking round?'

'No, no … not unless you count the two weirdos who called the other night.'

His slight menace turned to angry interrogation. He moved closer to Urinal, who instinctively moved back. So did the group. They had heard about the flood and the subsequent murders, and had put two and two together.

'Really? Do you know who they are? What did they ask? Come on, spit it out.'

'They run the building site in Throttle. That's all I know. We worked for them a while ago. They're OK. Nothing fishy.'

'Maybe I should pay them a visit, see what it is they want. But if I find out there's something you're not telling me…?'

Urinal gave a forced laughed. The others, sensing the threat, gave sickly smiles.

'Why would I lie? What's it to us what you get up to?'
'Meaning?'
'Nothing. We are up here. They are down there. We have no connection. We work hard for you, and we are grateful for the work.'

'OK. Let's keep it that way.'

***

Not too far away the hairs on the back of Reginald's neck began to stand on end. Having spoken to the gent on the phone before, he immediately recognised the gruff voice.

'It's him. He's there now. Come on,' he shouted, ripping off the headphones they were sharing.

'Who's he calling a weirdo?' added Simon indignantly.

As they scrambled from the van the four-by-four sped

past, showering them in muddy water. In the moonlight Reginald caught a glimpse of the profile of the driver.

'It were him, Big Dick … so close we could have grabbed him.'

***

Emma and Gareth, however, could make no sense of the conversation, and were just about to leave when a voice from another darkened room startled them. They squinted.

'Hasta la vista, baby,' the voice said.

They, unfortunately, had chosen the house that the workers used as a toilet. They turned to see a man with his trousers round his ankles waving a toilet roll in one hand and a torch in the other. They scrambled out of the house with the man shouting at them unintelligibly and waving his torch.

Outside of the perimeter of the site they stopped running to get their breath back. Gareth leant on his knees, gasping for breath, and said, 'Did we really get rumbled by a half-naked man shouting at us like Arnie?'

When they had regained their composure they set off at a more casual pace and walked back to Throttle. As they strolled they assessed the activity.

'The point is: have we gained anything? Having spent the last three hours in a freezing and stinking workman's toilet are we any nearer to knowing what's going on?'

'For "gained anything" do you mean either flu or diphtheria?' said Emma, trying to lighten the situation.

'Ha ha. Be serious. I think all this is taking its toll on me.'

'Well, it's a first for me. How about you?' she laughed.

'Be serious,' he said. 'We can't keep putting ourselves

in harm's way for nothing.'

'You've changed your tune. Yesterday you were all gung-ho. Now you're just gung. However, I have to say it's something I can put in my diary. But as for being helpful ... not a lot.'

'I'm not sleeping, not after the site hut business. I keep having nightmares about me sinking in a bath of wet concrete.'

Miles away from trouble and strife?

Roland sat in a large padded easy chair with a pot of fresh coffee accompanying a generous glass of brandy. As he looked through the stained-glass window across the Thames he could see the House of Commons all lit up and apparently vibrant with activity. Aware of the mayhem in Throttle, he thought he had better touch base with a colleague who might be able to help. After a few phone calls they arranged to meet.

'What the frig are you doing here? I've not seen you for years. In fact I've not seen you since the piss-up. You'll not remember much about that night, though.'

'I don't even remember the occasion.'

'I presume you've not come here for a tour. It's madness over there. There's more back-stabbing than in bleeding *Macbeth*,' said the man in a pinstriped suit, while pointing across the Thames.

'We have a little local difficulty. Someone thinks they have a right to threaten us. In fact ... so much so that they have wrecked a dozen houses and killed two local lads in the process, and I was hoping you could help to get to the bottom of it.'

'Me? How would I know?'

'Because I'm convinced that when we started this venture with the housing estate you said you would see if we could keep the cost down. You knew a man who could help… I'm just wondering, that's all.'

'"We"? The royal frigging "we"? All I did was oil the wheels of commerce.'

'Ah, that's what I mean. Whoever it was who got oiled now wants paying. I tell you they are homicidal nutters… They've killed two already. Come on, who is it?'

'I don't know anyone who would go to those extremes over a paltry debt.'

'Well, they have. They drained the canal and flooded the estate. Throttle is like a war zone. So who do you think *thinks* that we owe them a cut?'

'I'm not sure, but the point is… Do we pay them off, or put a stop to them?'

'Either way, it's not going to be pretty.'

The man looked at the clock, confirmed the time on his watch, threw his coat over his arm and waved goodbye.

'Don't worry. I'll sort it,' he added as he left.

Outside the man paused, wiped his finger down the contact list on his phone, then texted, *What are you up to, you bleeding idiot?*

Minutes later, his phone buzzed.

Trying to get back what I am owed, though it seems to have got out of hand, the text read.

You're not wrong there, get a grip man or you'll have us all eating porridge, he replied.

Questions need answers

During his afternoon tea break, John Costain looked at his phone. A text from Robert invited him to meet two friends who would be willing to help.

Can you come round after work?

Bit short notice, he texted back.

Do you want answers, or what? replied Robert.

'That was a bit curt,' John thought.

He rushed out of work, putting his jacket on as he ran. Normally he would call in for a swift pint on the way home.

'If I don't go for a pint I'll get home at the usual time, so she will be none the wiser,' he reasoned to himself.

He felt more familiar this time, and so did not knock on the boat from the embankment. He climbed straight on and rattled the door bolt.

'Hello,' he shouted.

Robert opened the door. 'Come in. I've some friends I'd like you to meet.'

They squeezed down the narrow passageway to the lounge.

'Hello,' John repeated, this time a little more restrained. 'Bookends,' he thought.

Robert pointed towards the settee where the two men were sitting.

'These are the colleagues who have offered to help

find the underlying cause of the problem of the asbestos.'

John stared at them. 'Friends, colleagues ... what are they?' he wondered.

Their appearance was the direct opposite of Robert's, with their cropped, slicked-back hair and dark suits. 'Straight out of *Men in Black*,' went through his mind.

'Hello,' he repeated.

'Yes. Hello, John. We would like to help you. It sounds as if you have a serious issue regarding ground contamination.'

John looked at Robert.

'How much have you said? I thought we were keeping this between ourselves.'

'All I said was that there is a problem about the land under your house, and that shady deals might have occurred in order to get permission to build it.'

'Your secret is safe with us, John,' one of the suits reassured him.

John, not feeling at all reassured, probed further.

'So what exactly is it that you do?'

'We are well practised in the art of gaining information. We have assisted many people in similar circumstances to you. We have the ability to gain access to details from individuals that, under normal circumstances, they would not be willing to divulge ... and we need your permission to carry on with the investigation.'

John was stunned.

'An investigation... Sounds a bit heavy.'

Robert could see the apprehension in John's face, so offered a thoughtful comment.

'Well, if you want answers and the means to move on in your life we need to put pressure on certain departments in order to find out who is responsible.'

'Well, aye, if you put it like that,' John agreed.

He looked at the two gents sitting opposite. They looked back with a take-it-or-leave-it facial expression.

He was caught in a quandary, but knew he would have to make a quick decision. His head hurt.

'I either put up with the house as it is, or get mixed up with Mr Strange and Mr Sinister,' he thought.

He naively asked a question he already knew the answer to.

'Are you sure this is legal? I mean … sorting out the land is one thing, but we don't want to get locked up for this.'

They smiled in a creepy kind of way.

'I can assure you that we are totally professional in what we do and, as a consequence, we do not intend to break any laws.'

'Just legs,' added Robert and laughed out loud.

John was struggling to see the joke, and Robert's comment confirmed his feelings.

'OK, we'll leave it with you. When you have made up your mind, let Robert know and he will contact us. Rest on it. But, like Robert says, if you want to move on…'

The two menacing gentlemen left first, then as Robert escorted John down the passageway he stopped outside the bedroom door and sought reassurance.

'Are you sure we are doing the right thing? Only this seems to be getting a little brutal for my liking.'

'Don't worry. Let them get on with it,' Robert said, ushering him through the door.

***

Afterwards Robert slumped into his easy chair. His face registered confusion and doubt.

'You can come out now.'

The inner cabin door opened. Sheepishly Linda Costain entered, partially dressed and wearing Robert's dressing gown.

'It's very posh in here. It doesn't look much from the outside. It's as though you're hiding from something.'

Robert looked at her, then played with his dreadlocks and looked away.

'I'm not sure about this. It's a bit too close to home. "Never shit on your own doorstep," my old dad used to say.'

She moved over and sat on the arm of the chair.

'Don't worry about him. He's too busy with his other problems. I'm a good wife and mother ... I spend all day cooking and cleaning.'

***

Later that evening John lay in bed reflecting on the day's events and watching his wife go through her ritual of night-time preparation: eyes first, then the overall application of moisturiser.

He sniffed the aromatic perfume.

'New is it, the body lotion?'

'Only got it yesterday. Do you like it?'

The lights went out. In the darkness he wondered where he had smelt it before.

Time to review the situation

It was that time of day again.

'Have you checked the builders in?' Reginald said, running down his list.

'Yes,' replied Simon, bored with the whole thing.

'Done the chart?'

'Yes.'

'Phoned the estate agent lady?'

'Yes. For frig's sake, let's do something physical instead of this admin shit.'

Reginald nodded and put the kettle on. Not much was being said until Simon broke the silence.

'We've heard him, we've spoken to him, we've even seen him ... but we haven't actually been able to get our hands on him. We need to get hold of the git.'

Reginald offered a word of caution.

'But do we want to get our hands on him? He sounds a bit of a rough bastard, if you ask me, and he can obviously handle himself. He has no concern for who he kills. He's a double murderer, and a home-destroyer to boot. It would be better if we could expedite the revenge remotely – you know, from afar. Then we wouldn't be implicated.'

Simon nodded, then looked up at the ceiling for support. 'We need to isolate him, give him some of his own medicine, and then hand him over to the authorities. You never know. We might get a reward.'

It was one of those uncanny coincidences. At the same moment as Simon mentioned the word 'authorities', a loud rap at the hut door suggested that it was from someone official, rather than someone wanting to borrow a shovel. They looked at one another then cautiously walked towards the door. Reginald lifted the latch, and the door opened to reveal two trench-coat-wearing members of Her Majesty's police force. Reginald offered a welcome.

'Well, hello, and who the frig are you?' he said, adding a small amount of cynicism to his voice.

Simon had had many run-ins with the police, and as a result harboured dark inner feelings towards them … feelings that were sometimes uncontrollable, and because of this he offered a less than welcoming greeting.

'What the fuck do you want?' he blurted out.

'Can we discuss this inside?' said one of the officers officiously as he held out his warrant card.

Simon closed the door behind them. The officer smiled as he attempted to lighten the atmosphere.

'That's better.'

'Now then, I am DC Spade and this is DI Digger.' They nodded to each other, but Simon was not placated.

'So?' he grunted.

The officer's face started to show frustration.

'Now look, we are investigating the double murder that occurred in the village, and we have information which leads us to believe that whoever did it was involved with the flood that damaged your houses. Correct?'

'It might be,' Reginald muttered, not wanting to commit himself.

The officer screwed up his eyes then added, 'Have I seen you before?'

Simon looked back at him hard.

'Maybe … possibly.'

'Can you not string more than two words together?' the officer said as he raised his voice.

Digger's eyes were everywhere. Then he focused on the coat rack on the back of the door. He elbowed Spade, then pointed and said, 'I knew we had. It's the black and white minstrels. You've made a mess of the barman. But don't worry: he won't split on you. He's shit scared you'll do the other leg.'

Then he observed the glazed door in the middle of the hut.

'What the fuck's this?'

'It's just a door, and none of your business.'

'There's been a double murder. Everything is my business,' he barked. 'Now what are you two up to?'

'Same as you. Whoever flooded the houses owes us a lot of money.'

It was then that Digger looked closer at the glazed door.

'I get it now. It's your version of an investigation board complete with sketches, a name and a number. Well that is interesting.'

'We have nowt for you,' shouted Simon as he smudged the information with the palm of his hand.

'Get in our way or conceal evidence and we will do you for it. It comes under the heading of "Obstructing a police officer in the pursuance of their duty". Understand?'

Simon looked at the black ink on his hand, wiped it on the back of his pants and stared into space.

The officers smiled, pointed at the coats and the glazed door and left.

***

As soon as they were outside Digger curled his lip and whispered, 'Did you get the number?'

'No problem.' There was a pause then Spade added, 'But what now? Are we just going to ring the double murderer and say, "Please come to the station so that we can arrest you"?'

Digger spotted the scepticism and sneered.

'It's a bit more technical than that. Believe it or not, there are people in our back room who can triangulate the location when the phone is being used.'

'Hey … clever.'

'Then, once we know, we set off and arrest him.'

Spade, who was having one of those glass-half-empty days, added further doubt to the plan.

'Let's say he's in a pub. Do we arrest the whole pub, or surround it? How do we know who he is?'

'It's a process of elimination. We know he's not a woman, not young, not old … in fact we are looking for a big rough-looking bastard in his forties or fifties,' added Digger rather smugly.

Spade beamed.

'Don't forget the mud. He will be covered in mud and, of course, he will have a phone in his hand.'

Then Digger's face slumped.

'Just like everyone else in a restaurant.'

The reporters report back

After having been summoned by the boss, the wily reporters recalled the efforts of the previous day. The editor listened, pointed at them then set about in fits of laughter. The reporters' expressions remained motionless, which indicated that they were not at all impressed by their editor.

'So let's see what we have. Well … not much, really. Not a story, anyway. You're going to have to dig deeper. Go and listen at that house again, at the estate office … and have another look round their hut. There is a story here, but we are going to have to put some meat on the very bare bones.

'Corruption: that's always a good angle. Let's see if we can come up with some evidence of dodgy goings-on. Building sites are full of corruption, not only from the owners and the developers – but who, where, and why did the land become available for building on? Then there're the planners. Have the developers followed the instructions given for planning, and for health and safety? The builders: are they proper employees? There's loads to go at.'

Emma, very unimpressed, looked at him. She looked around the office and noted the modern fittings and the view of the main street below.

'It's all right for you, sitting here in a centrally heated

office with your window to the world. There are serious nutters out there, who've got reputations for breaking legs and killing people.'

Gareth nodded. He was glad Emma had spoken out and stated exactly what he was thinking but was too afraid to say.

'She's right. We were lucky last time. We might not be next time. I'm not sleeping properly any more. I keep waking up and imagining that bloke with his hands round my throat.'

The editor held out his arms and tilted his head to one side.

'We don't want you to get hurt, so be smart and look out for one another. Go and get another bug in that shed – one that you can listen in to from a greater range.'

As he warmed to the idea, Gareth smiled just enough to show commitment, then rubbed his hands in acceptance of his boss's idea.

'It should be OK … if it's a longer-range gadget.'

Emma frowned.

'I'm still not sure about this. It still seems an easy way to get your face rearranged.'

In an attempt to resolve the situation the editor compromised and pointed at Emma.

'OK. You do the listening in, Gareth and I will do the dirty work. But first go and get a more powerful bug.'

A new plan

Simon and Reginald had done the rounds of the site, and were putting ticks against a wallchart indicating which houses were still damp and which houses could now be sold.

'OK. Things are moving,' announced Reginald in a positive way. 'But we now need to nail that bastard before the police do. If we catch him first the chances are that we can get some cash back against the cost of repairing the homes. If the police catch him we are snookered. They will just lock him up.'

'We can't go in empty-handed, though, can we? Remember, he has nowt to lose.'

There was a pause as Reginald considered his own thoughts and negativity crept into his mind.

'And, if we catch him, where do we put him? And how do we stop him from escaping? It's not going to be straightforward … big, tough bastard, this. It's a long time since we did any physical work, and this monster could do real harm.'

Simon tried to recollect the last time they were involved in any fisticuffs, and was struggling to remember anything of note.

'There was that bloke on whatsit street – you know, we did his back yard wall – but he were only small. Then the last one I remember was on that roof job – remember, we had our butties up there then came down and charged him for the time – but he were only a pensioner, and he soon coughed up.'

Reginald looked at his ever-increasing waistline, then studied the palms of his hands.

'We've got soft!' he announced as he looked for hard skin on his knuckles. 'We've been doing this soft job for so long now that we are unfit. We are incapable of pursuing our previous profession. What happens if we have to go back? The punters would laugh at being threatened by two fat blokes.'

Simon watched in amazement at his rant. Then he checked his own waist, then his hands.

'You're right. In that case we need the tools of the trade. We'd better visit the store … see what we need.'

***

It was ten minutes away by old white van. They arrived at a cobbled street flanked by rows of back-to-back terraced houses. They inched their way down a narrowback street. The construction equipment in the van rattled up and down as they edged over the cobblestones to a row of almost dilapidated garages. In the middle of the row a garage that seemed to be supported by those on either side was showing its age.

'It's years since we've been here. I've almost forgotten what's in it,' said Simon as he rummaged through a ring full of keys for the right one.

Rust stains ran down the front of the door from an enormous old chain, which was held together by a large padlock. Simon operated the key and lifted up the up-and-over door. Lights that were powered by a car battery were switched on, and the door was closed with a bang behind them.

Simon kicked a large chest and said, 'It should all be in here.'

They prised open the lid and gazed at the contents. Inside was an array of fear-provoking weapons: clubs, pickaxe handles, handcuffs and two quite rusty sawn-off double-barrelled shotguns.

'We never did use these... Just as well: they would probably kill the operator. They don't half frighten folk, though,' he added, pointing one at Reginald.

'Are you fucking mad? It could still be loaded.'

'Sorry. Sorry ... it still has that effect, though.'

He eased the stiff mechanism to break open the gun to check the breech.

'Good God. There's still one in it.'

Reginald grabbed the gun and pulled out the cartridge. It was a spent one. He threw it at Simon.

'Don't you ever...'

'I know. Sorry.'

There was a moment of reflection on the last five minutes, then normal service resumed.

'Going to keep him in here, are we?'

'I think it could be cosy.'

'Getting him here could be the problem, but I think I might have the answer.'

Reginald reached up to a glass cabinet and took out a small bottle with a rusty lid. He held it to the light and peered at the murky liquid.

'Does this stuff go off?' he asked, giving it a shake.

Am I dreaming, or is this a nightmare?

Joe Lagg awoke but thought he was still asleep – dreaming, that is – because although he had opened his eyes he could not see anything. Then he realised he could not move, either – although he did feel a sense of movement, as though he was rocking. As realisation dawned he started to panic, but could not shout. He was in fact tied, gagged and blindfolded.

'Don't panic, Mr Lagg,' said a voice from behind.

'You truss me up then call me "Mister", you bastards,' he thought.

'We just want some answers. I'm sure you can help.'

'We have been drafted in by a third party to speak to you … cos they can't stand the sight of blood.'

'If we can just introduce ourselves … we are communication experts, i.e. we get you to tell us answers to our questions.'

'We're very good at it,' said a voice from the opposite side of the room. 'Yesterday, in a warehouse not far from here, a chap just like you gave us what we wanted in minutes.'

'Now then, let's get down to business. This is how it works. I'm going to ask you a question, then I pull the rag from your mouth and you give us the answer. OK?'

The man looked at Joe.

'Then nod your frigging head, then.'

Joe obliged. His mind was racing.

'What could I possibly know that they would want?' he thought.

'Oh,' said the man, in apologetic manner. 'The reason we get quick answers, as per yesterday, is because of this. I know you can't see it, so I'll describe it. This is a three-hundred-watt electric soldering iron. It gets so hot you can smell it. Its official use is for melting solder, like when you're making stained-glass windows.'

'Very crafty,' added the other man.

'Do you know what I mean? If you do, nod your head.'

Joe nodded, and started to sweat.

'Oh, by the way, if you give us duff answers – you know, just to stop the pain – we will kidnap you again and the whole process starts over. Understand? If you do, nod your head.'

Joe nodded vigorously.

'OK. Your starter for ten... Did you know that the area you built houses on was contaminated with asbestos...? Think before you answer.' He leant towards Joe and pulled the rag from his mouth.

'No,' said Joe.

'Sorry, wrong answer. Plug the iron in, will you, please?'

The man stuffed the rag back into Joe's mouth.

'It's not going to be a record tonight. It's a bit of a bugger. There's some good stuff on the box,' he said to his partner.

'Joe, have a think as the iron is warming up... You know ... something might come to you ... cos I hate the smell of burning flesh.'

Moments later the iron started to warm up, but then the lights went out. In the total darkness there was a pause in conversation, then a spark of realisation.

'What's up?'

'A technical issue.'

'Go on.'

'Well, it appears that the 240-volt generator we are using only puts out one kilowatt: one thousand watts to you and me. Our iron pushed the demand to twelve hundred, so the generator tripped.'

The man holding the iron sought further detailed advice from his colleague. 'So let me get this right ... We can have the lights on but no iron, or we can have the iron on but no lights. So when the iron is hot I can't see where I am sticking it to him.'

'That's about the size of it—'

Joe started to scream through the gag in his mouth. It did not reach the two men.

'Which is unfortunate, Mr Lagg, cos normally we try to only affect people where in everyday life it would not show. But, as you can see, or not see – that is, if I can't see – I could affect you where it *could* be seen, if you get my drift.'

'Excuse us, Mr Lagg,' said the second man. 'We are going to see if we can solve the issue in order to prevent any facial disfigurement on your part. We won't be long, I can assure you.'

Joe started to shake and sweat even though it was chilly.

Moments later the two sinister gentlemen returned, smiling in the knowledge that they had overcome the technical difficulty.

'Now then, where were we? Oh, yes. I am sure you are happy that we have solved the problem of the power failure, Mr Lagg. We are going to torture you by candlelight. That way we can keep the iron at its maximum temperature and not worry about a loss in electrical power.

'So, let's start again. Did you know that there was asbestos on the land where you built the houses? Nod or shake, if you like.' The man moved closer with the candle. 'Make your answers more definite. It can save you a lot of pain.'

Joe relented and nodded.

'Good. Right answer. Now a bonus point. How did you get planning permission to build the houses? Think hard.'

He pulled the rag from Joe's mouth.

'I didn't have anything to do with the planning permission. All I do is just sell them.'

'Oh, dear. It's answers we need, not excuses.'

The man moved forward to reinsert the rag into Joe's mouth.

'Roland. It must be Roland,' Joe shouted.

'Can you smell the heat of the iron? That's because it's awfully close to you. Go on with your answer.'

'Roland ... he does funny handshakes with them at the golf club.'

'Funny hands with who?'

'Them from the council.'

There was a slight pause as they discussed the answer. They shook their heads.

'No, sorry. We need more: names, positions, departments ... that kind of thing. You can think on it while we warm up the iron.'

The sinister men, who were carrying candles, went into the next room. Joe heard the mutterings, but could not make out the conversation. In the cold, dark – and now rocking – empty room he could take no more.

'That's all I know. They play golf, one of them is an MP and they're from the council.'

He did not remember anything else. There was just a short struggle as he fell asleep.

***

A while later he awoke. He was lying on the back seat of his car, and he had a blinding headache. He paused for a moment. First of all he couldn't understand why he was on the back seat. He sat up, then wondered about the funny odour, the bits of cotton in his mouth … then the remnants of the sticky tape on his wrist. He flopped down onto the seat as the 'dream' reappeared in his mind.

***

Roland had spent a pleasant day in London. He was leaning on the barrier between himself and the Thames and staring down at the dirty brown river water when a light went on in his head. It was his conscience. It had never bothered him before, but all of a sudden he felt the need to phone Joe Lagg to see if all was OK. After all, he was at the sharp end … and there was a lot going on.

'Hey, hello. I was just wondering how you're doing. I know it's been rough just lately.' After what seemed an age he asked, 'Hey, are you still there?'

Through tear-stained eyes Joe managed to control himself enough to communicate, though the manner of his communication took Roland aback a bit.

'Do you know what somebody wanted to do to me yesterday? Well, I'll tell you. They wanted to shove a hot iron into me,' he screamed. 'All because of those poxy houses we built on your dad's mill. They said that if I didn't tell them how we got permission, they would stick a hot iron into me where it won't show.'

Roland was stunned. He expected drama because that was Joe's way, but this was different.

'So what did you say? You're obviously at home right now.'

'Don't worry. I didn't drop you in it. I just said we paid somebody at the council.'

'And that satisfied them?'

'You don't believe me, do you? I was drugged, tortured then drugged again. I'm not frigging well dreaming. I was abducted, tortured then left in the back of my car, where I woke up.'

'So what did they actually do to you? Have you been to hospital to get the burns sorted out?'

'Well, they didn't exactly do anything, actually. Once I told them about the council they let me go, but if I hadn't told them about the council they said they would have stuck a hot iron into me.'

'So you said. Are you sure you didn't tell them any more? It seems strange to go to all that trouble then just let you go.'

'So would you be happier if they had burnt me? Then I would have had something to show for it. You don't believe me, do you?'

'Of course I believe you. Look, I'm getting a train back soon. I'll come and see you.'

Doubt crept into his mind about just how many beans Joe had spilt. Then, as he put the phone away, he sniggered.

'I might have to stick a hot iron into him to find out.'

Bug number three

In the editor's office they read the instructions of the new listening device, then Emma asked a simple question.

'Is this legal? I mean ... are we encroaching on a person's privacy?'

'Good point. Would they sell them if it were illegal? I think it all boils down to whether you get caught or not.'

Gareth tried to clarify matters.

'If the person you are bugging is committing a bigger crime than you are committing by using the bug ... does that not wipe out the illegality of using the bug?'

'It's a bit of a bugger if you ask me,' Emma sniggered.

'OK ... according to the instructions we have to place this device as close to the source of the conversation as possible, and without a barrier between the bug and the source. What do they have in their site office that would serve this purpose, on the basis that we need to be in and out of the office, not looking round for a place to put it?'

They cast their minds back to the time they were there and went through all the appliances in the office, but none seemed suitable.

'I can't think of anything. Then, of course, we have to get in. We were fortunate last time – and, as I recall – they have one hell of a padlock on the door. And it hasn't got to look like a break-in.'

Gareth's facial expression went from that of a person

who has not got a clue to one who has just discovered the answer to the world's problems.

'What's the shed made of? The answer is wood, so why don't we just drill a hole in an inconspicuous place and push the bug through?'

'Neat idea. Now you're thinking,' Emma said supportively.

They drew a plan of the site office from memory, then decided on where X would mark the spot.

'Hole size?' asked the editor.

'A good inch,' replied Gareth as he held a ruler against the bug.

'OK. It seems easy enough. We'll go for midnight. We'll need a torch, a plan and a cordless drill. Let's meet here at eleven.'

***

The following day Emma sat in the back of the *Throttle Flyer*'s delivery van with a rucksack full of sandwiches and a flask. She had a notepad and pen at the ready, just in case it got complicated. Listening intently was OK for the first hour, but hearing them discuss building details and everyday happenings at a building site became tedious for her. As the time dragged on she ended up doodling and trying to plan her escape from the *Throttle Flyer*, an endeavour that was becoming increasingly near the top of her to-do list.

She had got the job because nobody else had applied. Initially she was very excited to be offered the post, and to be given the title of *Throttle Flyer* reporter. The pep talk on her first day indicated that the career structure allowed individuals to start at the bottom of the ladder and work their way to the top unhindered. After a few weeks it dawned on her that the only way to the top was to marry the chairman – and he was already married, he was sixty plus, he was overweight and he had a beard.

I'm not keen on beards, so that's a non-starter, she wrote. Then underneath she added the real reason. *The hours are long, the pay is paltry – and now, on top of all that, I'm expected to put my very existence on the line.*

'Well, not for much longer,' she thought.

***

In the site office cum shed cum investigation department Simon was planning the next move, but ideas were a bit short on the ground. He rubbed his hands together.

'Is it cold in here? Bit draughty?' he asked.

Reginald, who was sitting at his own desk in a cosy corner, offered an unsympathetic response.

'Not especially.'

'Well, it's bleeding cold over here.'

As he put his hands under the desk to rub his cold legs he felt a distinct draught.

Not willing to put up with the discomfort any more, he got down on his knees and searched for the source of the draught. When he discovered the reason the disbelief made him jump. There was a bang as his head hit the underside of the desk. Despite being taken aback on discovering the cause of the chill, he crawled out on all fours and crept over to where Reginald sat.

'They're at it again,' he whispered in his brother's ear.

They stepped silently out of the office, climbed into the van and stared through the windscreen.

'It's got to be them bloody reporters. Full points for persistence, but what are they expecting us to say that's going to be any use to them?'

Simon began to laugh.

'Wouldn't it be nice if we could kill two birds with one stone and introduce the *Throttle Flyer*'s best to Dick the murderer? The hunted becomes the hunter: the poacher becomes the gamekeeper,' he added in a voice usually reserved for advertising thriller films.

'The garage could be the rendezvous. It's got lighting, it's got security and it's very snug.'

'So we have to get Dick the killer and them reporters to go on a wild goose chase – or, in this case, a garage chase – and get them to meet at the same point … scare the shit out of them.'

'We need a lure, we need a trap … and we need to get even.'

A man's gotta know his limitations

Graham had had a couple of days rest since Albert arrived, and was feeling more peaceful towards the world. Neither the police nor Simon and Reginald had been back. This he was grateful for, but the unknown factor was that Dick the murderer had not made contact either.

Over lunch he confided his fears.

'It appears that I am the only one who has actually seen him. I am the witness to what he did, and guess what? I even showed him how to use the bleeding controls.'

Albert tried to sympathise.

'That doesn't implicate you at all. You were only doing somebody a favour. You are not responsible for what he did. You are just an innocent bystander, like the rest of us. Remember, if it wasn't for him my boat wouldn't be on its arse and I wouldn't have spent a week in hospital – not to mention being ridiculed by all and fucking sundry by having my picture in the paper, so…'

At this point Albert took a long slurp of his tea, exhaled and went on.

'We need to be ready if he calls—'

'This *if* business …' interrupted Graham, 'wouldn't it be better if we could predict when he calls, rather than just wait? After all, how long do we give it? A week, a month, a year?'

'I see what you mean – and while we're on the subject, I have a small debt to settle with them at the fucking *Throttle Flyer* – so if we could kill two birds with one stone I would appreciate it.'

Over another brew they were each lost in their own thoughts, then Graham laid it on the line.

'There's a simple principle, using the country way of doing things. You give them a reason to fall into your trap.'

'Reason? What kind of reason?'

'You have to appeal to their basic instincts. His life revolves around money, and them at the *Throttle Flyer* live for a scoop. By the way, I have been watching you struggle with that old Ferguson. Sorry to ruin the illusion about classic tractors, but it's way out of date... Come this way.'

They walked to the barn, then through the back into another garage. Graham stood in front of what appeared to be a pile of straw and pulled on the corner of a huge tarpaulin. As the straw fell away and the tarpaulin rolled to the ground it revealed a shiny new yellow digger. Albert's lower jaw almost hit the floor.

'I thought that—'

'Nobody asked. The police assumed he'd taken it with him. It seemed too good to give away – so I hid it, in part payment for all the hassle.'

'Got the key?' asked Albert.

***

In the next village Simon and Reginald assumed their evening shift in their van, and started listening in to the goings-on in the builders' accommodation.

Simon sighed. 'It's like listening to *The Archers*, only

in a foreign language.'

Reginald exhaled loudly as he contradicted Simon's words of wisdom. 'So how can it be like *The Archers* if it's in a foreign language? And, what's more, *The Archers* is about country life – living on a farm, and such.'

Simon was not convinced.

'It's an everyday story of country folk, but they're not saying which country.'

'No, you pillock. It's an everyday story of people who live in the country as in *fields*, not an everyday story of people who live in *different countries*.'

They were just about to go round in circles again when a four-by-four blazed past and slid to a halt in the mud outside the builders' accommodation.

'It's him,' whispered Simon, as though he could be heard.

***

Across from the road in another house Gareth and the editor heard the car, and peeped through an unfinished window.

'It's him, I think,' said Gareth.

'Who?'

'Him … the man they're all afraid of.'

In the house the conversation got heated between Urinal and Dick. They were arguing in Polish and being watched by the other builders. It was then that the eavesdroppers got lucky.

'Speak in English,' Richard grunted. 'We don't want these fuckers knowing our business.'

'It's the men. They think they are being ripped off. They were promised proper accommodation, not living like this. And if they are to stay here they want more money, and I don't blame them.'

'If I thought you were putting these men up to this I'd rip your fucking head off.'

Meanwhile, on the other end of the bugging device, everyone grinned. 'Trouble at t'mill,' whispered Reginald.

Then Richard left in a hurry.

***

In the darkness of the van they discussed the next move.

'He's not having it all his own way, then. The point is … what has he done with the money that was supposed to be for accommodation?'

'He's put it in his back pocket,' they said in unison.

'I wonder if the man who gave him the money knows.'

***

In the other house the editor and Gareth were trying to make sense of what they had heard.

'It sounds like he's fiddling them,' they decided.

The pit and the pendulum

Meanwhile, down on the farm, the intruder alarm – as Albert affectionately called the great trap – was taking shape.

After climbing a narrow metal ladder up to the highest point, Albert peered through a small sight window into the gloom of the huge manure silo. It was located conveniently between the shippen and the field. He could not see much, other than the fact that fluid was halfway up the tank.

'Don't strike a match. It'll blow thee to kingdom come,' Graham shouted from below.

Albert's face formed an expression which suggested that he was not aware that he might be wiped out by such a small act.

'Really?'

'It's full of methane gas,' he explained.

'I knew farms were dangerous places, but I never would have thought this … it's a gasometer. In the wrong hands it's a bomb.'

The farmer went on.

'It's not been touched for about three years … should be nice and mature by now.'

'Mature manure … got a nice ring to it. I like that,' said Albert.

***

In the car park round the corner from the estate agent's, Emma listened in to the everyday goings-on in Joe Lagg's office. 'Tedious and mind-numbing' was a phrase she was beginning to use frequently, so after one such three-hour period she flipped the headphones off and informed Gareth that she'd had enough for one morning and that she was going shopping.

As she climbed out of the van she turned and got back in.

'I've just seen 'em … Lagg and the two thugs from the building site. They've just gone into the office.'

She replaced the headphones and sat, pen and pad at the ready.

'Can you hear what's going on?' asked Gareth on his mobile.

'Clear as day,' she whispered as she listened in. 'Lagg's got a stutter. He sounds upset,' she told him.

In the office, Joe Lagg related the episode of the torture to Reginald and Simon. They did their best to keep a straight face.

'So I want you to get them, and kill them if you have to. Knife the bastards who did this to me,' he shouted, then demonstrated the act of knifing somebody several times.

Emma lifted the headphones away from her ears in disbelief.

'I must apologise. At some point I remember saying that this was a ghost town, and nothing ever happens here. Two murders, a torture session … and now incitement to murder, previously unsolved deaths and arson. What a place.'

The editor had become aware of the excitement, so he rushed out of his office and sat beside her in the van. He

took her pen and wrote in large letters on her pad,
None of it solved.

***

Not very far away, Simon and Reginald were sitting in their van.

'I'm afraid he's cracked up, and he wants us to do his dirty work. If we do what he asks and get caught … it's us who'll go down, not him. Of course, we know the two weirdos who did it, don't we? Not many round here enjoy their work as much as those two.'

Simon, who up to now had just been nodding approval, added his thoughts. 'Site managers, detectives and now revenge administrators. We're going to be busy.'

***

About ten miles away in a town very similar to Throttle, the lights blazed from a small stone-built pub on the main street. They walked in, but avoided the bar. Instead they went straight to a round table in the middle of the room that was occupied by two very smartly dressed men.

'Hello, guys… We believe you've been busy.'

Simon stood behind one of the men and rested his hands on his shoulders. As he attempted to rise, Simon pressed him back down. The landlord had been watching and got fidgety. He turned and reached for the phone on the wall. Reginald gave him some advice.

'It's OK … just a friendly chat. No need for that.'

The landlord offered a thin smile and replaced the receiver.

'Good lad. Now four pints of your best, if you don't mind. Over here, when you're ready.'

All was silent until the beer arrived. Most of it was

spilt by the trembling hands of the landlord.

Simon raised his glass.

'I give you a toast to GBH and corruption. Long may it continue. Come on, don't be miserable.'

The others muttered the toast and put down their glasses.

'I'll bet you're wondering why we are here,' added Reginald with a mocking laugh in his voice. 'It seems you can't stick to your own patch, but we will ignore that for the moment. You see, your last assignment affected a close colleague of ours – affected him so much that he wants us to stick you with big knives – but we will ignore that also for the moment. The thing is … we need to know who put you up to it. Now I know all about customer confidentiality, but you owe us big time.'

'We do not snitch on clients. It's bad for business. No one would hire us if they thought we couldn't keep it shut.'

Simon, who had his back to the landlord, leant forward and pulled at the lapel of his jacket. A big shiny knife handle was exposed.

'You remember the sticking with big knives order, don't you? We are prepared to ignore it, but not for long. So you stick to your own patch, OK?'

To be or not?

John Costain had spent a few restless days wondering about the connection between his wife's body lotion and the similar scent he had detected in Robert's boat. He had considered confrontation, but then he also considered the awful row if his suspicions were wrong. After all, it would not say much for their relationship if he were to put it at risk over a simple 'similar odour' situation.

So he decided to spy on her. There was no other word for it. At the same time and on the same day of the week when he had smelt it first, he decided to see if he was able to smell a rat again. He positioned himself far enough away in the undergrowth not to be seen, but close enough to observe and to recognise any individuals who might be coming and going.

What he did not bank on was the canalside neighbourhood watch person, who was also equipped with binoculars and a phone.

'Robert, there's a bloke in the woods spying on you. He's been there about an hour. I don't recognise him.'

'Cheers, Harry. It could be someone from the waterways or something. I'll have a look-see.'

Robert tentatively poked his binoculars through a gap in the curtains. He focused the lens, then gasped. 'It's your bleeding husband,' he said to Linda.

'Oh, my God. What are we going to do?' panicked

Linda as she pulled the bed sheets up to her neck.

'We can't do anything till he leaves. Otherwise the game is really up.'

She looked at her watch. 'He must have left work early. He doesn't usually get home till five… That gives us another hour, then,' she winked.

However, the thought of having relations with a woman whose husband was only feet away caused Robert to go off the idea. Linda sulked.

'How did he know? And how can I talk to him knowing that he does know?'

The time dragged on, and eventually John got cold and wondered if he was doing his wife an injustice in suspecting her of infidelity. Robert kept watch and as soon as John had disappeared out of sight Linda dashed home, taking a shortcut across a football field.

On his way home, he had time to reflect. 'He's a mate of mine. He wouldn't … would he?'

By the time he arrived home Linda had assumed the role of devoted wife and mother by taking care of the washing-up. With her hands in the sink she turned, smiled and carried on as though she had been there all day.

'Hi. Had a good day?' he enquired.

'Oh, you know. Just the usual.'

As he was hanging his coat up he noticed that Linda's shoes were covered in mud.

'Get out today, did you?' he asked in a prying way.

'Oh, you know … just to the shops.'

It was then that he noticed a smear of black paint on the cuff of her coat.

He heard Robert's voice in the background. 'If you own a boat you are constantly bleeding painting.'

Promotion or redundancy

The editor of the *Throttle Flyer* had been summoned to a meeting with the board of directors. He casually climbed up the grand staircase and let his hand follow the highly polished and bulbous balustrade. He glanced at framed old front pages with emblazoned headlines:

War Declared

'There's nothing new … it could have been printed yesterday,' he thought as he passed. As he walked through the tall oak door he was ushered to a seat and given an agenda. He scanned the sheet but, being a one-item agenda, there was little else to read. After the usual pleasantries and the vote to agree the minutes of the last meeting, the chairman stood, cleared his throat and read out the one item.

'The future?' he proclaimed, and returned to his seat.

'I see you've put a question mark at the end of item one,' the editor remarked.

'That's because at the moment there is uncertainty,' replied the chairman.

Chastened, the editor sat silently.

The board members looked at one another, and then the secretary coughed and said, 'Shall I begin?'

The others nodded.

'Times are hard. We used to make money from the sale of the papers, and people would queue to buy them.

But not now. We rely on the income from advertisers which, up until now, has worked well. We could always rely on the good nature of local firms to place big adverts. High street shops would always place ads, and even the situations vacant column on a Friday would attract customers. But now ... local firms are going bust, job vacancies are a thing of the past – and, if we don't watch it, so will we.'

'Jesus,' gasped the editor.

No one else said anything. They just stared at him.

'Hey, don't look at me,' he added, and held out his open palms.

The chairman stood up and said, 'We would like to show you a simple graph. It only goes back a couple of years.'

He switched on the computer and fiddled until he got the graph on the screen large enough to be seen.

'This shows paper sales.' He pointed with his pen. 'As you can see, there is a series of spikes. They are all above this horizontal line, which indicates survival. Sales have to be above this line or we close. These spikes can be related to certain news items: murders, arson, floods, scandals, riots, etc.'

They all turned to face the editor.

'I'm sorry, but our future relies on you… It's up to you to ensure that the sales are above this line.'

'No pressure there, then,' was the editor's parting shot as he left the meeting.

The following day the editor cascaded the information to his trusty reporters, who said, 'But you said we weren't to make up stories. Look what happened to the last reporter,' said Gareth.

'I did… Things have changed.'

Roland ventures out

Roland had decided it was time that he sorted out his life, so whilst in London he took the opportunity to test his mettle where he thought he could do no harm. He was confused; his exterior was that of a lively person who did not have a care in the world, but inwardly he was disappointed with the way his life was working out. He was bored, had no interests or hobbies and yearned to meet interesting people.

'Fat chance of meeting anyone interesting in Throttle.'

However, in London he felt even more isolated: of the hordes of people, none knew him or cared about him. Strangely though, he had a plan of how to put this right. He had been online and acquired membership cards for a gentleman's club and a singles club. So with the details safely tucked away in his case, he booked in at a five-star hotel on the Thames Embankment.

'Business or pleasure?' the receptionist enquired as she filled in his registration card.

'Oh,' he stuttered. 'Depends how it works out.'

'Breakfast between seven-thirty and ten, he will show you to your room, enjoy your stay,' she rattled off officiously.

He turned to find a bell boy already carrying his bags towards the lift. Roland hastily followed then they waited for the lift to arrive.

'Room number?' the bell boy asked as the doors opened.

Roland turned over the large brass key fob. 'Four-o-five' he replied as they stepped in. They reached their floor and as the doors opened, they stepped out onto a blandly decorated corridor.

'This way,' said the boy, setting off at a pace. They passed door after door until they found the room. Roland looked back towards the lift, which appeared to him to be a long way away.

'How many rooms did you say?'

'Forty on each floor and there are six floors.'

Roland swiped the card several times before the lock opened, then stepped in.

'I thought this was advertised as personal and intimate.'

The boy said nothing, shrugged his shoulders, dropped the bags and paused near the door. Roland pulled back the curtains then turned to see the boy standing there.

'I was promised a view of the Thames… Here,' he said, holding out a two-pound coin.

'Thanks,' said the boy, dropping his affected smile.

***

After two days of isolation, the receptionist went to Roland's breakfast table and enquired about his state of mind.

'Are you OK?' she said whilst pouring out his morning coffee. 'Only we are a bit worried about you.'

'Who's worried?'

'We are, we have been watching you. The "Do not disturb" sign is permanently on your door – the cleaners don't want to disturb you, but they need to do their job.'

'Well, thank you very much for your concern, but I am OK,' he said, looking down at his full fried breakfast. 'Oh, and since you have been watching me, what conclusion did you arrive at?' he added.

'Nothing really, other than that you are probably escaping, like all the rest.'

'Escaping from what?'

'Could be anything – tedium, life crisis – we get many people here who are escaping.'

Then his phone whistled. He read the display, saw it was Joe so pressed the off button.

'Tell me again,' he said, resting his chin on the palms of his hands.

'Oh nothing, it's just that, you know, spending all that time on your own sitting in your room, not eating properly, there's a case conference there.'

Thinking that he needed to offer an explanation, he tendered what he thought would end the conversation, but he just made it worse.

'I've been doing some research, that's all.'

'Tell me more,' she said, pulling up a chair.

'Your other guests, won't they need attention?'

'No, Jordan over there will see to that.'

Roland turned to see the bell-boy, wearing a different uniform, pouring coffee.

'It's not really research, it's just that I've got to attend a few do's and it's not something I'm used to, so I have been swotting up.'

'So, not scientific or technical research then?' she said glumly.

'No, more how to overcome the nerves of chatting … speaking to strangers … the fear … you know, so you don't say the wrong thing.'

'Chatting, as in chatting up?'

'Yes, chatting, as in small talk.'

She sat up, her mind pondering the issue, then suggested an alternative to his confinement.

'I might be able to get you a head start, that is, after you have finished your *research*. Have you ordered a meal for tonight?'

'Meal ... not thought about that.'

'Well you should, it's a way of supporting life.'

He offered a thin smile and nodded.

'I can help you find a place if you like?'

'Not much fun eating on your own – I tend to graze.'

'Graze?'

'Eat as you go, if you know what I mean.'

'Think I do ... it sounds a bit lonely.'

'Exactly that, but the alternative is difficult.'

'You are in Greenwich, the place is buzzing, loads of places to eat, let me help.'

Later, the receptionist rang his room.

'Hello Mr Bullock, I hope you don't mind, but I've booked you a meal for seven o'clock. If you come to reception about six-thirty, a lady will show you the location.'

'Really? OK.'

The following morning he awoke in his hotel room. He felt strange. He had a splitting headache. And then he realised he was not wearing any pyjamas.

'I never go to bed without pyjamas,' he pondered.

He sat up and his head started to spin. He felt wobbly so he closed his eyes and the spinning began to slow down. Having calmed down, he looked across to the desk where his personal effects were placed. He quickly scanned the area. 'Watch, wallet and card holder, all seems OK,' he mumbled. Then he opened the wallet; all the cash was gone, replaced with a hand-written note:

I took some nice pictures of you. If you want the SIM card to have a look, £500 should cover it. Phone this number soon or you will see them in a tabloid.

He sat on the edge of the bed and thought deeply. After a coffee and some pills, he rubbed his face to aid the recovery, then smiled.

'What a dummy,' he laughed loudly.

'Reginald, I need a favour. Put on your best suit, drive to the hotel and interrogate the receptionist, Lydia I think she is called – oh, and I've a number for you.'

Reginald responded immediately by trying on a suit he had not worn for ages.

'Simon, I have to go to London to rescue Roland. Be a pal, whilst I have a shower, unpick the back seam of these pants a bit so that I can breathe.'

'No problem – does this mean I am in charge and can make decisions of national interest?'

'Yes, it means you can decide how many sugars to have in your tea.'

After a long drive to the hotel, Reginald stretched his legs in the car park then walked through the reception area and into the café. He was trying to be casual but could not help but notice that people were staring.

'The Italian style of this suit always commands respect. It gives the wearer confidence,' he thought.

He sat in the coffee lounge and beckoned a passing waiter. As he arrived, Reginald looked at his badge.

'Jordan, how are you?'

Startled at this unusually familiar question, Jordan replied, 'Fine, I think.'

Pleasantries over, Reginald went straight in.

'Lydia, the receptionist, when does she start? I believe she has a smart blue car.'

'No, it's a red Alpha, and she starts her shift at two.'

'Thank you very much! A pot of breakfast tea for one please.'

Positioned in the car park, Reginald waited for Lydia to arrive. He looked at his watch then back to the entrance. Bang on time for her shift, a small red Alpha Romeo cruised in. She adjusted her position in the parking bay, then Reginald, who had started the van, slowly moved towards her. Still sitting in the driving seat, she felt a bump as Reginald scraped the front of her car. Looking the other way, Reginald drove to the furthest corner of the car park, opened the back doors and waited casually. Now irate, Lydia stood at the front of her car taking photo's of the damage and then, waving her arms aloft, strutted over to the van. The moment she arrived, without saying a word, Reginald pushed her straight into the back and shut the door. Minutes later she found herself with hands tied to a rail used for securing building equipment. He watched as she regained her composure then turned on the interior light and clambered between the front seats to confront her.

'As you can see, I am fastidious about being neat and tidy, all these tools are in their place. It's called a shadow board – if an item goes missing I know about it right away. This axe, for instance, went missing once. I knew about it right away because all I could see was its shadow, get it?'

She nodded nervously.

'And as you can see, saws, hammers and crowbars, all in their place, nothing lying around that could make it untidy.'

He paused a moment then carried on.

'Do you like your job being a receptionist? Being a receptionist, I think you would have to have a presence. Now if you lost, let's say, your ears or your nose, your presence would be gone. You could still exist, of course, although it would be awkward wearing glasses, and it would probably affect your social life... Now then, down to business. My boss says you got him this escort who took photos of him naked in bed. I think it's hilarious but he doesn't see it that way, and he pays my wages. Anyway, your friend the escort now wants £500 for the pictures or she will go public... I'll bet you are wondering where all this will end.'

She nodded then tried to explain.

'I told her it was just an escort job but she thought he was an easy touch and she went too far. I don't get anything out of it, I just thought it would be a good idea,' she blubbered.

'Yes well, some friends you can't rely on – her details, now!'

Reginald noted the address then set the Sat Nav, and a while later they drove into the car park of her friend's apartment block.

'Very nice. Must be a good earner being an escort, maybe I should become one?'

He turned to Lydia, who had stopped sobbing, and outlined the plan.

'It's simple: to put all this to bed and get you back behind your reception desk, we need the SIM card with the photos on, but she won't come down to the van if I ask her, but she will if you do. Tell her you have the details of another client but you need to hand it over in the car park.'

Reginald looked at the car to his left then continued.

'Tell her you are in the Mercedes next to the white van.'

He held the phone to her face as she made the call, and seconds later he spotted the escort coming out of the front door. As she got close to the Mercedes, Reginald grabbed her and pushed her into the van alongside her friend.

'He says he is going to cut my ears off if we don't give him the photos,' Lydia ranted.

Reginald held out his hand. 'Phone please?'

The friend rummaged in her bag then held out the phone. Reginald swiped the screen then touched the gallery button.

'There's loads here, all naked men, asleep in bed. What a system you've got. At £500 quid a shot, no wonder you can afford to live here.'

He swiped further until he found the photos of Roland.

'There we go, very nice. You are good at this, no missing heads or fingers across the screen. But unfortunately that's as far as we go. So, I take the SIM card out and put it in a safe place. If, of course, you feel hard done by and want to go to the police, I will show them the contents, then you two go down for a long time – blackmail is a serious offence.'

He flicked out the SIM card, dropped the phone to the floor and stamped on it, then opened the back doors of the van.

'Go,' he said bluntly.

He drove back to the hotel and met Roland in the foyer.

'Here,' he said, smiling and holding out the card. 'Do you want a lift back home?'

'You are joking, I've not had as much fun for ages, but you can take me to another hotel. Just one other thing, you do know you are showing your arse?'

'I thought it was draughty. I was in a hurry, so while I was in the shower I got Simon to free up the stitching. No lower than the jacket I told him. He's hopeless.'

Another day, another gruesome plan

Now that Reginald was back home after his trip, he and Simon were considering the most opportune moment to nail Dick the murderer. They had decided to carry the shotguns, even though they were not loaded. Reginald eased the stiff mechanism open and peered down the inside of the barrel. Instead of shiny rifling, all he could see was corrosion.

'It's best if we don't fire them. I don't think they're safe to use … just use them for frightening purposes.'

'Suppose he calls our bluff. What then? Do we throw them at him?'

'Let's hope it doesn't come to that.'

Simon, still not convinced, sought clarification.

'So let's get this straight. We ambush him, give him a dose of this then take him to the lock-up. Is that right?'

He held up the small bottle containing the murky liquid and shook it. The disturbed sediment made it even cloudier.

'Do you think it gets stronger as it evaporates?'

He unscrewed the lid and brought the bottle close to his face.

Reginald watched in disbelief.

'You are not going to sniff it, are you?'

'What, me? No.'

It was too late. He quickly put the lid back and held

it out. Reginald took it from him as he sat down with a bump.

'You really are stupid. This stuff knocks horses out. We got it from a vet.'

Simon shook his head and opened his eyes wide to aid his recovery.

'Are you OK?' his brother enquired.

'Yeah, I think so. It was just like being hit over the head with something heavy.'

'Got a rag?' asked Reginald.

'Why?'

'We need a rag to put it on. If you're going to dope him you can't just pour it over him.'

***

They thought it out again. The plan was to get the reporters and Dick the murderer to arrive at the garage simultaneously by offering information that would appeal to both parties. After Simon had fully recovered they sat on the floor cross-legged, adjacent to the desk, and placed the phone next to the bug to ensure the reporters would hear properly.

'OK. Ready when you are,' Simon whispered.

Reginald dialled the number then, script in hand, waited for the phone to connect. Seconds later a recognisable gruff voice answered.

'Hello.'

'Hello, it's me. We need to talk.'

'Who *is* me?'

'Don't talk in riddles. You know who we are. You wrecked our houses, and we would like compensation.'

'Really? You'll get more than compensation if I get my hands on you.'

'We are not going to let you get away with this. We will follow you everywhere till we get paid.'

'Really?'

'We know all about you – who you are, who you work with and what you have done – and if we don't get any compensation we will pass it to the police and let them find you.'

'Are you phoning from a bathroom? It sounds strange … a bit wooden.'

'Never mind that. We need to meet.'

Dick was beginning to think this was too easy. First of all he was being threatened, then they were arranging to meet him – where, presumably, he would have an opportunity to silence them.

While listening in to all this Emma was jumping up and down with excitement in the van. With pen at the ready, she was poised to write down the details.

'Let me get a pen… OK, come on then, where and when?' Dick asked.

'OK. On the edge of town, just off the bypass, is a group of houses. Round the back is Slack Street. There is a set of garages. We will be outside the middle one at eight tonight.'

'Garages, Slack, at eight,' Dick said as he wrote.

'Garages, Slack, at eight,' wrote Emma. She ripped off her headphones, gathered her belongings and ran to the office.

Dick, however, had a concern. 'It seems too easy, this,' he thought.

Emma rushed upstairs shouting, 'It's on. It's on!'

They knocked on the editor's door.

'Yes? Come in,' he said.

'It's on tonight … the meeting… The murderer will

be there.'

'You're going to be busy, then, aren't you?'

***

Emma and Gareth had discussed this prior to seeing the editor, and had decided that this rendezvous needed someone with more experience … someone who had dealt with this situation before … someone who was paid a heck of a lot more.

'Er, we have decided to back you up, but it's you who should be witnessing the meeting,' Emma said. 'We will be there as backup, of course, but this is a meeting between two thugs and a double murderer… It's way above our pay grade.'

'I see. A long-lens camera is needed.'

'Well yes, but you have to witness it closer – obviously, not too close – just close enough,' Emma asserted.

***

In the site office Reginald and Simon continued to make everyday noises and inane conversation, even though nobody was listening. When it came to discussing the meeting, they sat in the van.

'On the basis that Dick is going to be there, what is the plan?'

'We will have to play it by ear, but I reckon we frighten him with the guns and get the better of him, then put him to sleep. Then when he wakes up he should be in no position to refuse to get us the money. He must have loads after diddling the builders.'

***

The editor was having reservations about the meeting, and had decided that as it was going to be dark – and in an unlit alleyway – an all-black outfit would serve him best in order to blend into the background. Dick, on the other hand, had already been round to reconnoitre the location, and decided that if he got there early, a disused outside toilet would give him cover until he decided what action to take.

***

Thirty years of dampness had affected the old metal box in the garage until the bottom had completely rusted away. At the bottom of the box, under a pile of offensive weapons, was a wooden tray containing twelve hand grenades. The previous owner (who also had owned them for thirty years) had replaced the corroding lever-releasing pins with nails which, as a result of the dampness, had now become rotted replicas of their former selves.

At the allotted time Simon and Reginald had decided to hide either side of one of the other garages and, with rusty guns at the ready, were preparing to ambush Dick as he arrived. Dick, though, was already there, sitting on the seat of the long-drop toilet and watching through a gap in the lavatory door.

***

The editor, quaking a little, was still sitting in his car round the corner. He had given the arrangement a lot of thought, and was now having second thoughts. It had dawned on him that if he got mixed up with either party he could easily end up in hospital.

'I had better observe from a distance,' he said,

fumbling with a camera.

'Getting cold feet, are we?' Emma said mockingly from the back seat.

'You'll be fine. Just keep your head down,' added Gareth, smirking.

Emma looked at her watch and urged him out of the car.

'You'll be fine. Remember, we are here if you need us.'

He got out of the car and cautiously sneaked down the back of the garages. Keeping quiet was difficult due to the long grass and accumulated rubbish and, in the darkness, treading on dry undergrowth was difficult to avoid. As he made his way he lost count of the garages, and wondered where he was.

In a moment of madness he decided to gently tiptoe to the front of the garages, where he could get his bearings. He stopped just short of the end and put his head round the corner. All of a sudden he was gripped in a headlock with a rag of chloroform over his mouth.

'Got him, got him,' shouted Simon as he supported the now limp body.

They dragged him to their garage and propped him against the door. Reginald stood back from him and weighed up his stature.

'Dick's a big fucker. This isn't him.'

'Oh. OK ... what now?' asked Simon casually, not at all bothered that they had chloroformed the wrong man.

'Bung him into the garage till the real Big Dick arrives.'

They shuffled him to one side to allow Simon to undo the lock on the chain. As he inserted the key, the editor started to recover and struggled with Reginald, who was trying to hold him. Simon then let go of the lock and chain to aid his brother.

The resultant clang of chain and lock against sheet metal door created enough vibration to disturb the now delicately poised hand grenade pins. The shock turned the corroded pin to dust, and released the lever. As the lever flicked out, aided by its spring, it disturbed the one next to it – until, one by one, all the levers were activated.

Five seconds can seem a long time when you are waiting for the kettle to boil. Unaware of this time lag, the struggle continued, and it was fortuitous that they were wrapped in each other when the flash and boom lit up the night sky and most of the village.

The lucky circumstance of being on the other side of the sheet metal door was lost on all three when the enormous explosion blew them and the door across the street. Simon and Reginald were found by the fire service under the crumpled door, still clutching the editor and their sawn-off shotguns. The blast destroyed the other garages and set fire to the cars parked inside, with the exploding petrol tanks adding to the confusion. A crowd gathered to see what was happing, and various theories were put into plain words.

'It's a bit bleeding early for Bonfire Night,' pronounced one neighbour.

'Terrorists, got to be terrorists,' announced another.

'So why would terrorists want to destroy a knackered old garage?'

Two mackintosh-wearing individuals had their own theory.

'What do you think, Spade?'

'Nutters. The place is full of nutters. What goes on in these garages would make your hair curl – and, don't forget, this *is* Throttle.'

As the casualties were stretchered away a jovial

ambulance man made light of their injuries.

'You were bloody lucky. The door saved your life.'

A heavily bandaged Reginald could not reply.

***

The shock of the blast had affected others not far away. Dick staggered into the street after having made good use of his hiding place, though he wished that he had disrobed first. Wide-eyed, he coughed and spluttered. And then as the dust settled he made a hasty retreat, mumbling as he went, 'That was meant for me. They don't mess about, these bastards.'

***

No formal reason was given by the fire services as to the cause of the blast. It was therefore classified as a bomb that had gone off in the making. As the police searched the cordoned-off zone they found to their amazement that the area was littered with handcuffs, pickaxe handles, knives and guns of all kinds. As a constable carried the weapons to a police van he offered a different take on the incident.

'There was some serious sexual deviance going on in that garage,' he sniggered.

***

At the foot of a hospital bed Digger and Spade made enquiries, and at the same time tried to stifle their laughter.

'Who's behind the green door?' Spade whispered melodically, and added, 'Frankie Vaughan, 1957.'

'Frig … off,' replied Simon.

'Oh, look. It's a gangster, peppered with his own shrapnel. Going to club someone to death with your gun, were you? That's all it was fit for … it had more rust than a Citroën.'

'Just … frig off.'

Simon turned away and watched his heart monitor rise and fall as he wondered where it all went wrong.

***

Back at the *Throttle Flyer* the topic of discussion between the reporters and the management was swaying from sympathy for the blast-affected editor to euphoria about the fantastic photos of the explosion site and the prospect of selling loads of papers.

'I could take this when we go visiting… I'm sure he will be pleased,' Emma said, while holding a copy of the front page.

I've had enough…

John Costain was having a bad time with his domestic situation. His wife's obvious unfaithfulness had come out of the blue, and he was mystified as to how his visit to Robert's boat had prompted her to get mixed up with him.

'But it has to stop,' he told her firmly.

On the other hand, the problem relating to the asbestos contamination had taken a turn for the better. News had leaked out about the issue, and as a result of a deputation of householders barricading the planning department, a meeting of all concerned had been arranged. The desire from the council to keep a lid on the scandal had pressurised the planning department to seek a scapegoat relating to the original planning application and to offer the person early retirement.

At the meeting, the clamour from the residents was for heads to roll, and for compensation. This, however, was not on the table, and was not the remit of the council representatives. Nonetheless, to present a proactive approach to the circumstances, the council described a plan of sampling every patch of open land in the area – including gardens and drives – to look for asbestos hot spots. Assurances were given that if any contamination was found, a team of appropriately clad technicians would be drafted in to remove and replace any suspect soil.

The affected householders, now reconciled by the arrangement, nodded in agreement – and as a result, the meeting finished early. So, after smiles all round on the steps of the town hall, John set off to break the good news to his wife. He ran all the way, only to find her not at home.

'She went to the shops ages ago,' his daughter told him, without taking her eyes off the television.

The expression of elation on his face lasted only seconds, and instead became that of a cuckolded husband.

***

In times of boredom he had thought about this moment. What would he do if this apparently adulterous state of affairs came to a head? He decided that the evidence was overwhelming, and there was only one course of action. He raced into the garage and collected a small hessian sack, and then walked purposefully to the canal embankment.

He approached Robert's boat, put down the sack and stared. In the stillness he listened intently. Just to make sure he wasn't making an awful mistake, he leant closer to what he believed to be the bedroom window. His worst fears were realised as he heard the carnal moans of his wife and the grunts of his so-called friend.

'That's it … you bastards,' he shouted.

With his mind made up, he carefully twisted some stiff wire through each lock on the outside of the boat.

'OK, so far so good,' he told himself. 'That should keep them where I want them.'

He climbed onto the back of the boat and attached a very long drill bit to a cordless drill. He was not aware of what was beneath the deck board. It was just that by his calculations the drill should be long enough to go clean through the hull. Even though he was putting all his body weight against the drill, the process took longer than he expected, primarily because – unbeknown to him – he was drilling through all kinds of paraphernalia associated with the running of a narrowboat. Every time the drilling broke through another component, the drill jumped further down.

'It'll not be long now,' he said through gritted teeth.

The accompanying noise associated with drilling caused the lovemaking to pause.

'What's that?' Linda said.

'Don't worry about that. It will be Harry on the next boat. He's always doing something.'

As John continued with the drilling, from the corner of his eye he noticed that he was being watched. He turned to see Harry – the occupant of the next boat – sitting cross-legged on the embankment, engulfed in a cloud of blue smoke from a very large joint. Grateful for a rest from the exertion, John stopped drilling and offered a compliment.

'That's a big one,' he said.

'It's for sharing,' Harry said, and offered him the joint.

John did not need asking twice. He lifted the drill out and laid it flat on the decking. He sat alongside Harry and took a long, slow drag on the joint. It took his breath away, brought tears to his eyes ... and then made him smile.

'Frigging cracker, this,' he croaked.

'Home-grown ... always the best.'

Harry pointed the joint towards the boat. Then, between coughing fits, he asked, 'What are you up to?'

'Just putting the shits up them.'

'The water's only eighteen inches deep.'

'She doesn't know that.'

'Who?'

'The wife. That's her in there, the one he's screwing.'

They both took another drag, and their smiles became wider and wider.

'Go on, then,' Harry urged.

John stepped out of the cloud of smoke, climbed back on the boat and continued drilling. Within minutes the drill gave way as it pierced through the metal hull. Water dripped from the end as he retrieved the drill bit. He turned and pointed to the water on the end, and they both set about in fits of laughter.

Meanwhile, unaware that they had limited time, Robert continued taking advantage of John's wife.

***

Robert had done well for himself, even though he had dropped out of university early. His studies took a back seat as he became more and more involved with a radical organisation that took drastic measures in matters of the environment and animal welfare. He showed such enthusiasm that he was offered a paid post by an underground movement. His job was organising demonstrations and protests in relation to anything from GM crops to the testing of products on animals. This lasted a number of years, until he became disillusioned at the increase in physical violence required to achieve their objectives.

It was a fortunate coincidence that, at the very time he was considering quitting, a relative who had followed his exploits died and left him a substantial sum to be put towards his militant organisation. He bought a boat instead.

His father was fully aware of his son's gift of the gab. His obvious good looks and the sympathising female support for his activities meant he was never short of female companionship.

'But if I can give you one piece of advice, son, it's this,' said his father. 'Don't crap on your own doorstep.'

This fatherly guidance would reappear in his mind time and time again on inconvenient occasions.

'He is a friend. This is wrong,' Robert blurted out uncontrollably.

Suddenly their lovemaking stopped, and the ability to perform temporarily deserted him. Linda, confused by this sudden lack of activity, sensed his anxiety and noticed his blank expression.

'He is dumping me a second time,' she mumbled to herself, as anger filled her head. 'I'm going to the bathroom,' she said.

'Fine,' he replied curtly.

As she stepped onto the floor the chill of cold water coming up through the floorboards startled her.

'We're sinking,' she screamed as the cold hit the soles of her feet.

Robert pulled back the curtains and observed John and Harry sitting on the canal bank smoking another joint. He shook his head and slumped back onto the bed.

Meanwhile Linda had grabbed an axe from the fireplace, and run back to the bedroom. Holding the axe aloft she stood in the doorway, naked, red-eyed and dripping, and offered a prediction.

'We are going to die… We all will drown if we don't do something.'

Robert stared.

'What a lucky escape,' he mumbled.

***

After smoking two joints John was feeling tired and ready for the off. He turned to his new friend and asked a technical question.

'The boat's ruined, then?'

'Oh, no. If he blocks up the hole tomorrow, pumps it out and leaves it to dry it'll be fine, then couple of weekends fiddling with it will sort it.'

'That's OK, then. Do me a favour... Let them out in ten minutes.'

He collected his belongings and, unsure of the future, set off down the canal towpath...

***

At the farm Albert and Graham were getting anxious.

'We have to get him to turn up, else we sit here forever.'

'Or they take us by surprise ... in the middle of the night,' chipped in Graham as he gripped the twelve-bore.

'Aye ... well, aye,' said Albert as he took it away from him.

Graham was in a philosophical mood.

'I can't carry on like this. I've got to put this little lot to bed and get on with life.'

'Well, we are ready for him. So here: dial the number and invite him.'

'What, just like that?'

'Well ... you want him here, don't you? Tell him to get here at six o'clock ... sort everything out.'

He took the phone, dialled, then paused.

Dick was not well, he was still feeling the effects of the

explosion, the ringing in his ears and the headaches had not gone away, so he was a bit short on patience.

'What?' he barked.

'It's me, Fossit.'

'Ah, Mr Fossit. I've been meaning to pay you a visit to thank you for all your assistance.'

'Like as if… Anyway, I've got something of yours, so if you wouldn't mind coming to collect your belongings… I'm at the farm, and if you don't come soon I'm off to the police. We know what you've done.'

'Really? Police? OK, well … that puts a different slant on it.'

'So when will you be in, then?' he smirked.

'Six tonight. OK?'

'OK. I'll be there.'

As soon as Graham had come off the phone he went for the gun. Albert had spotted his move, and also grabbed the gun. They struggled, and eventually Albert wrestled it from him.

'The double murderer is on his way. Give it to me,' he screamed.

***

Dick stuck a finger into his ear and wriggled it. It did not help to calm the ringing in his head.

'Bastard,' he said as he popped more pills out of their bubble pack. 'But, hey, things are looking up. I got shut of the two weirdos. Now I am going to sort out two other birds with one stone: the digger and the paperwork … and I'll sort out Fossit at the same time … grand,' he thought out loud.

***

In the back room of the police station, frustration set in.

'The calls are still not giving us enough time to pinpoint the whereabouts,' a communications technician advised them.

Digger and Spade had their trench coats at the ready for any action.

'We've got to be patient. It's a waiting game … I can feel it in my bones. There's going to be some action soon.'

***

Dick phoned his boss.

'Hello, it's me… That little matter we have to sort, up at Fossit's farm … it's today. Where are you?'

'As in "sort out", do you mean "further fatalities"?'

'I've told you: they were accidents. But this needs sorting. It'll be just a cosy chat. Anyway, where are you?'

'Leeds. That hotel near to the station.'

'OK. I'll be there about half five.'

***

In the police station, nerves were getting on edge as the technician missed out again.

'Can't you put all these calls together and get a fix? This is getting ridiculous. We are so close.'

At six p.m. Dick pulled up outside the hotel.

'The traffic's shite… Hurry up. Get in. We are going to sort the last witness.'

He threw the man in like a rag doll, who then sat up and replied, 'What do you mean by "sort out"?'

'What the fuck do you think I mean? "Sort out", as in, "Make sure he can no longer tell anybody".'

'You used the word "body", as in "deceased". You're already a double murderer. You're going to be a triple murderer.'

'Aye, and you're a triple murderer's accomplice.'
Albert started to suspect that they had been double-crossed when Dick missed his deadline. He threw Graham the phone and the notepad.

'Here, ring him… Let's see what he's up to.'

Graham squinted through his glasses as he pushed the buttons.

'Where the frig are you? We said six. It's nearly seven now. You'll have it dark.'

'Hang on. I got stuck in traffic, but I'm on my way now. I'll not be much longer.'

***

In the police station, excitement grew and thumbs were raised.

'I've got him. He's on the Old Throttle Road.'

Digger and Spade faced each other.

'There's nowt else up there but Fossit's farm. Let's go.'

***

All was quiet as the car approached. Albert had already opened the gate to entice him in.

'Where are we?' said Robin, the accomplice.

'Just some old bastard who can't keep his mouth shut's farm.'

Albert and Graham spotted the headlights, and decided to creep out round the back. Graham was shaking.

'I think my heart is going to jump out of my chest,' he said, panting deeply.

Inside the car Dick leant forward over the steering wheel. All was in darkness.

'Are we supposed to go and knock on the bleeding door? This is not a social call. There's something up here.'

Dick pressed the accelerator gently, and the car crept further along the track until it approached the house. Then it stopped.

'The frigging car's stopped,' Albert shouted to Graham, who was standing next to him.

'We have to get him closer. It won't work otherwise.'

Graham, unaware of Albert's plan, gave him a funny look.

'Sorry, Graham, but drastic measures, etc…'

Albert bundled Graham out into the open and into the glare of the headlights. Dick saw them and crept a fraction closer.

Robin the accomplice panicked.

'He's got a frigging gun – a big gun,' he yelled.

Graham rested the twelve-bore across his arm and dangled a bunch of keys.

'Come on, you bastard, if you want these.'

Albert sensed a stand-off, and took the initiative. He pushed Graham towards the car.

'Are you fucking mad? He'll run us over.'

'No, he won't. Shake the keys. Dangle them out to him.'

Graham held out the keys. Dick seethed, and put his foot to the accelerator.

'What are you doing, you nutter?' shouted Robin.

'This should be easy. I'll run the git over … just another accident.'

Robin, however, did not see it that way.

'There are two … you'll be a quadruple murderer.'

'Shut the fuck up,' Dick grunted as he put his foot down hard on the accelerator.

He never noticed the straw-covered shit trap. In the darkness it looked just like the rest of the farm. The car lurched forward, then dipped down as the front end entered the pit. Dick slammed it in reverse but as the engine submerged under the brown liquid it stalled, and the car slipped slowly into the pit.

It floated for a while. Albert and Graham moved closer, and watched the level of the liquid rise up the side of the car and the panic going on inside. As gasps of air belched from underneath, the car sank further and further.

Graham's mouth fell open as he watched the spectacle.

'When did you dig this?'

'While you were asleep. I used that posh new digger. It didn't take long. Then I emptied the slurry tank into it.'

The car floated for a while before sinking completely. And then it rested on the bottom, with just the top surface of the roof visible.

Albert folded his arms, smiled and smugly announced, 'It was only a rough guess, but I appear to have estimated the depth of the pit bang on... Just deep enough to swallow a car.'

Graham was changing his mind about Albert.

Minutes later Digger and Spade arrived, and they too looked down onto the roof. Digger's phone rang.

'We've lost the signal,' the technician informed him.

'I don't think it matters now.'

He turned to Albert and Graham, 'What is that God-awful stink?'

'Very old shit,' Graham informed him.

The police, the fire brigade and the ambulance services wondered who should sort this out. All were reluctant to volunteer.

Digger spelt it out.

'There're two men in there, who are probably still alive. For frig's sake do something.'

'Like what?' they shouted, not knowing what to do.

They all stood looking down, shaking their heads and holding out their hands. Then all of a sudden a huge belch of air erupted and splattered them all in the mature fluid ... and two shit-covered heads rose, gasping for breath, from the pit.

***

As in all matters of this kind, the media appear to have a sixth sense when a situation like this happens, and they manage to arrive almost as quickly as the emergency services. The *Throttle Flyer*'s wily reporters pushed their way to the front, hoping for a front-page photo. Albert seized the moment.

'Can I have a look?' he asked, pointing to the expensive-looking camera.

'I suppose so, but be careful. It belongs to the paper,' the young photographer said reluctantly as he handed over the camera.

Albert took it, then without hesitation pushed the lad into the pit alongside Dick and Robin. He went under initially – and the others, in total shock, could not believe what he had done.

'Don't worry... It's only four foot deep. He'll be up in a minute.'

Sure enough, seconds later the lad stood upright, covered in manure.

Albert pointed the camera.

'Got you, you bastard,' he said, and smiled.

***

About the Author

Colin Goodwin enjoyed a successful career as a welding and fabrication engineer, working for the past twenty years in further education, where he also taught stained glass window making.
Recently retired, he is continuing to indulge his creative side by repairing anything mechanical (motor bikes, cars, model steam engines) and released his debut novel *Don't Get Mad Get Even in 2015*. Colin lives in Lancashire.